THE
EMPANADA
BROTHERHOOD

Also by John Nichols

Fiction
The Sterile Cuckoo
The Wizard of Loneliness
The Milagro Beanfield War
The Magic Journey
A Ghost in the Music
The Nirvana Blues
American Blood
An Elegy for September
Conjugal Bliss
The Voice of the Butterfly

Nonfiction
If Mountains Die (with William Davis)
The Last Beautiful Days of Autumn
On the Mesa
A Fragile Beauty
The Sky's the Limit
Keep It Simple
Dancing on the Stones
An American Child Supreme

THE **EMPANADA** A NOVEL
BROTHERHOOD

JOHN
NICHOLS

CHRONICLE BOOKS
SAN FRANCISCO

Library of Congress Cataloging-in-Publication Data is available.
ISBN-10: 0-8118-6052-3
ISBN-13: 978-0-8118-6052-9

This is a work of fiction. Names, places, characters, and incidents are products of
the author's imagination or are used fictionally. Any resemblance to actual people,
places, or events is entirely coincidental.

SOME NOTES ON LANGUAGE AND PRONUNCIATION
Argentines commonly use *vos* instead of *tú* as the second-person pronoun. Their
singular present tense and imperative verb endings correspond roughly to the plural
vosotros of European Spanish. This changes "normal" spelling and placement of
accents, confusing people outside of Argentina.

The command *dale*—"come on," "let's go"—is pronounced "*dah*-lay." The bitter
tea *yerba mate* is "yerba *mah*-tay." A *piba* is a lovely young woman. And *che* is a
vocative used to call attention, loosely meaning "hey," or "you," or "hey, you."

Lyrics to the tangos that appear in this book were translated by the author. Page 9,
"Anclao en París," lyrics by Enrique Cadicamo, music by Guillermo Barbieri. Page 52,
"Ríe payaso," lyrics by Emilio Falero, music by Virgilio Carmona. Page 100, "Cuando
tú no estás," lyrics by Alfredo Le Pera and Mario Zoppi Battistella, music by Carlos
Gardel and Marcel Lattes. Page 195, "Adiós muchachos," lyrics by Cesar Vedani, music
by Julio César Sanders.

Manufactured in Canada
Designed by Adam Machacek
Typesetting by Janis Reed

Distributed in Canada by Raincoast Books
9050 Shaughnessy Street
Vancouver, British Columbia V6P 6E5

10 9 8 7 6 5 4 3 2 1

Chronicle Books LLC
680 Second Street
San Francisco, California 94107
www.chroniclebooks.com

To Áureo Roldán

Oh how I yearn for your gentle caress!
Here I am stranded without money or friends.
Who knows but one night I'll be captured by death . . .
Then it's 'Ciao,' Buenos Aires, I'll never see you again.

—From a tango sung by Carlos Gardel

Contents

Cast of Characters

1. A Woman Scorned

Around ten P.M. one evening in early October a taxi veered to the MacDougal Street curb and a woman got out. Adriana, Eduardo's ex-wife, stumbled on her way over to the empanada stand but a college kid wearing a CCNY sweatshirt caught her. Adriana shook him off irately. She was almost thirty, a few years older than Eduardo, and wore red high heels and a raincoat. Her hair was fetchingly tousled. She had a thin erotic face that was twisted in anger.

"I'm looking for Eduardo," she said in Spanish. "Where is that bastard?" Her words were slurred from drinking and she delivered them with a phony Castilian accent.

"He hasn't been around tonight," Áureo Roldán explained politely. He was the cook at the stand, a fat man from Buenos Aires. In fact he owned the business, which was right in the middle of Greenwich Village between the Hip Bagel and the Figaro coffeehouse. "I haven't seen Eduardo for a couple of days," he said.

"You're lying, jefe. I know he comes here all the time. He's a prick and I want to kill him. He ruined my life, he brought me to this stinking country, and now I'm all alone and I can't function because I'm so upset and I hate him."

Adriana burst into tears. She put her elbows on the stand's window ledge facing the sidewalk, buried her face in her hands, and really sobbed, all the while excoriating Eduardo in language unbecoming to a female. Luigi slipped out of the narrow alley inside the smoky cubicle and put his arm around Adriana for comfort. But when he touched her she reacted as if a lightning bolt had struck, and, lurching away abruptly, she lost her balance, pitching onto the pavement.

Alfonso and Popeye raced from the kiosk to help Adriana. But she got up quickly, shaking her finger at Luigi, who was a little guy with cauliflower ears and terribly burnt features. She yelled, "Stay away from me you ugly jerk!"

Her face was already streaked with mascara. Alfonso said, "Calmate, vos. Nobody here wants to hurt you. We're sorry about the divorce."

"No you're not," she hissed back at him. "You men are all alike. You *enjoy* hurting women."

Then she turned around and teetered into the street, waving for a taxi.

Her sudden arrival and departure provoked a philosophical discussion among us about suffering: Who hurts more in a relationship, the man or the woman? Alfonso said, "The man does, but you don't see it. We hide our emotions. Women yell and scream a lot, releasing all the tension. That's why they live longer."

"But we treat them like dirt," Roldán said, scooping an empanada from the grease bin and putting it on a paper plate set on a skinny counter between the alley and his cooking area, which was barely five feet square. The entire kiosk was only eight feet wide and seven deep. The empanadas Roldán sold were small fried pies filled with beef or cheese or pork, or quince and raisins. You could also buy soft drinks, pastelitos, and thimble cups of dulce de leche.

"Women deserve what they get," Gino said. "That's their role in life." Gino sometimes worked at the kiosk on Roldán's night off. "Except for American chicks," he added. "They are so spoiled. I think American men are hopeless."

Popeye was prematurely bald and had tattoos of big-breasted pinup girls on his biceps. He said, "I love the minas, and if they want to play I'm their guy. I've spent all my money wenching and I don't regret a penny. But if they start to cry? It's sayonara. I love pussy but I won't tolerate sorrow."

Luigi remained silent, steaming in his own juices.

"What do *you* think, blondie?" Alfonso asked me, wiping his horn-rimmed glasses clean. He was a mathematics genius getting a doctorate at NYU.

I smiled. But what could I say to my new friends about this topic? At twenty-one and just out of college, I was very shy and still a virgin. It was the early 1960s, with no sexual revolution yet. Women to me were half demons, half angels, pitiless and exquisite, utterly mysterious and unapproachable.

2. Rich Gigolo

Popeye double-parked a diaper truck nearby and came over to the kiosk accompanied by another guy I hadn't met before. The sliding window facing the sidewalk was open and Popeye put a dollar on the ledge. Inside the kiosk, in the cramped alley, Alfonso, Carlos the Artist, and I were watching a movie starring Jane Russell and Clark Gable on Roldán's portable TV lodged on a shelf above the coffee machine. Carlos had straggly hair and a handlebar mustache. He fancied himself an existential Dadaist and worshiped Jean Cocteau.

Popeye ordered a yerba mate for himself and a hot chocolate for his sidekick.

"I have a new job," he proclaimed. "Who wants to buy my nylons?" The boys pronounced his name "Po-PAY-shea." Popeye pronounced his own name with a lisp because he lacked his four most prominent front teeth. He had once been a sailor in Argentina's merchant marine.

Alfonso pointed out, "The sign on that truck says 'Diapers.'"

"I sell nylons very cheaply, that's why I drive a diaper truck. This is my friend Chuy."

Chuy greeted everyone and immediately began to talk about himself. He had an effeminate face, and his blond hair was cut in a pageboy. He had arrived stateside to have surgery done on his arm after losing his hand in a car accident. His own true love had been killed in the crash that robbed him of his hand, so naturally he was a sad man. When he felt really morose he took it out on other ladies. Chuy had a quality the pibas adored, he couldn't explain exactly. But they fell hopelessly in love with him at first sight. To relieve his personal sorrow Chuy fucked these women until he felt happier again. If the minas were plentiful he only remained sad for short periods. Right now he had a half dozen girls on a weekly rotation taking care of his blues. The reason so many miserable men lived on this planet was that very few of them had balls the caliber of Chuy's. "Tanto cojo las minas que tengo orquitis."

Alfonso said, "Che, get out of here, you're stinking up the kiosk with your ego."

Chuy bristled. "Wait a minute, profe. You're stinking up the kiosk with your envidia."

Carlos the Artist said, "Leave us alone you miserable buffoon. We're watching television."

"I can see that," Chuy said. "Jane Russell? This must be a circle jerk."

At that moment a pretty girl wearing Bermuda shorts strutted by walking a miniature poodle. Chuy whistled and dashed from the stand, following her.

"Carajo," Alfonso grumbled to Popeye. "Where did you pick up that bag of manure?"

"He's very rich," Popeye said. "He has millions. He doesn't even have to work. And what he says about his success with women is true. He has a book filled with their photographs. He can get you introductions for free. They're all good girls and friends of his. I think we should be nice to him even if he's a creep and that missing hand gives us the willies."

Just then a person the size of a mouse arrived at the sidewalk window wearing a black leather jacket, baggy jeans with rolled-up cuffs, and red Converse All-Stars. Eddie Ortega was an errand boy for some local shady characters. He had a crew cut and a little mustache. Roldán punched the NO SALE key on his register, removed a few bills from the drawer, and gave them to the Puerto Rican gofer who made a cryptic entry in his pocket notebook.

After Eddie slithered off Alfonso said, "I think all the Chuys in the world should be locked in iron cages and hung from gibbets. I have no tolerance for that type of parasite."

Roldán immediately poured us free coffee refills in honor of gibbeting those bad Chuys.

3. Humiliation

The muchachos disliked Chuy for poking his book of girls in front of their noses, but nobody could refuse to look. Chuy commented salaciously about this piba or that chica—girls, girls, and more girls. How could a man as oily as Chuy be that successful with them?

According to Alfonso, "It's his filthy money. Also they feel sorry for him because of that hand."

Carlos the Artist agreed. "You always see beautiful women with cripples."

Luigi said, "The more you're a louse the more they spread their legs."

Carlos said, "With your face, Luigi, you should have a dozen muchachas crawling all over you."

"My burned skin is too much for them." Luigi took a small bottle from his pocket and squeezed drops into his eyes. "It strikes fear instead of sympathy."

Speak of the devil. Chuy arrived at the kiosk with a statuesque snob on his arm who acted like Greta Garbo. She wore a black pants suit, sunglasses despite the night darkness, and was smoking an English cigarette. They stayed at the sidewalk window because the rest of us had filled up the narrow alley for patrons inside the cubicle. It would have been polite to move out of the alley for Greta Garbo, and normally Alfonso would have initiated the gesture. But the snob had put him in a petulant mood so he didn't budge.

Roldán said, "Caballeros, there is a lady outside on cold pavement in the wind."

The lady was from Venezuela. She barked at the cocinero: "I can handle it, tubby. Give me a chicken empanada."

"Make that two," Chuy said, taking out his wallet and filtering through a bunch of twenties before he procured a ten and slapped it down expansively. We couldn't take our eyes off this crisp bill which had emerged from such a fat stack of cash.

"Wait a minute," Alfonso said. "Your money's no good here. Take it back. I'm buying."

Chuy said, "Don't patronize me, profe. You're always broke."

From his own billfold Alfonso removed the only piece of foliage, a ten-dollar bill. He set it on the counter between the alley and the grease bin.

"I insist," he announced grandly. "Nothing is too good for my friend Chuy and his novia."

"I'm not his fiancée," said Greta Garbo. "I'm his accountant."

"Order two empanadas apiece," Alfonso said derisively. "Live it up while you're still young."

The cook wrapped the empanadas in napkins, put them on paper plates, and placed the plates before Chuy and the accountant.

Chuy caught Alfonso by surprise by saying, "Thank you, we accept your gift with pleasure."

Now there was nothing for Roldán to do but scoop in Alfonso's sawbuck. He rang it up on the till and delivered the change, carefully counting pennies into the professor's palm. You could tell he was sorry to see a man as broke as Alfonso being one-upped by a braggart like Chuy.

The rich gigolo said, "You think you can insult me but you can't." He bit off the top of his empanada, shook in Tabasco, and took a hefty bite. "Mmm, this is *good*."

Then he fetched the book of photographs from his brief-case and leaned through the window, extending the album over the grease bin toward Alfonso.

"Anybody you want, profe. Just tell me. I'll make the introductions."

In English, Alfonso said, "When snowballs melt in hell, you punk."

Carlos the Artist eagerly grabbed the book and opened it. Luigi and I also gave it our undivided attention. Carlos turned a page and my heart stopped. There was a girl wearing a flamenco dress with a ruffled hem and poufy shoulders; a flower decorated her dark hair. She was young and pretty and insolent. The hands raised over her head were twisted dramatically and she glared at the camera with sexy anger.

Chuy noticed my expression. "That's Cathy Escudero, blondie. Do you like her?"

Luigi wondered, "How can such a precious kid wind up in a book like this?"

Chuy said, "She's a foul-mouthed guttersnipe but one heck of a dancer. If you want to meet her just say the word. She's only nineteen."

He devoured his empanada with exaggerated gusto, licking his manicured fingers, and promptly ordered another for himself and also for the accountant. That was too much for the professor who demanded to be let free of the alley. When we emptied onto the sidewalk he stormed off in a huff, completely humiliated.

Chuy wiped his mouth with a napkin. "Mirá, che, that was a good empanada!" he called after Alfonso. "Gracias!"

"Mine was great also!" yelled Greta Garbo.

4. Horns for Eduardo

Eduardo worked on documentary films and commercials for a local Spanish-language television station. He wore a Brooks Brothers suit and a gold stickpin in his tie. The shirt was button-down and striped, very elegant. Shiny patent-leather shoes completed the uptown outfit. But tonight he seemed loaded and his eyes were red from smoking marijuana. He stood on the sidewalk at the window sipping hot coffee as he complained angrily: "I think my wife, Adriana, is seeing another guy. If she is I'll kill her."

Roldán said, "Excuse me, but aren't you two divorced?"

"Of course. I couldn't stand her. I'm glad to be rid of her. But that doesn't mean the slut can go around making me look bad by dating other guys. I'm not going to wear the horns because of that bitch."

"They aren't horns if you're not married," Popeye pointed out from the alley. "Relax, nene. Babes are a dime a dozen."

"If it feels like horns to me it's horns," Eduardo insisted. "And it feels like horns. So I am going to kill her."

Luigi said, "They'll put you in jail. This is America. You can't erase your ex-wife for a crime of passion and get away with it."

"I don't care. All of New York City is laughing at me. I saw them enter her apartment building yesterday. He's fat and ugly, a real pimp. Her bad taste is a personal insult to me."

Alfonso said, "You're wasting your time, man. You divorced her so forget her."

"I can't forget her," Eduardo groaned. "Before we got divorced she bored me to tears. I couldn't stand the sight of her. All I wanted to do was be with other women. But the minute that judge signed our divorce decree Adriana became like a cancer in my heart. It's eating me alive. I'm going to strangle her with my own hands."

Roldán laughed. "If you do, blondie here will write a book about it. And you'll become a famous buffoon in the United States."

Eduardo glowered in my direction. "If blondie writes a book about me I'll strangle *him* with my own hands."

Hastily, I said, "I'm not going to write a book about you, I promise."

Luigi said, "She isn't worth it. You're lucky to be free."

Eduardo sneered, "What the hell would a burnt face like you know about women?"

Luigi eyed Eduardo thoughtfully for a moment but decided not to hit him. Instead, he told Roldán, "Give this moron another cup of black coffee." He clacked a quarter onto the counter:

"I'm paying for it."

5. Smitten

On Halloween night I arrived at the empanada stand around eleven P.M. after my stint washing dishes at the Night Owl Café. Half a dozen customers were eating pies while leaning against parked cars nearby. Werewolves, hobgoblins, and Frankensteins still crowded the Village sidewalks. The air smelled like Neapolitan pizza and Italian sausages. Taxicabs honked impatiently in the traffic jams on Bleecker and Mac-Dougal. Roldán wore a Lone Ranger mask and a cowboy hat. He had taped black cardboard bats and orange jack-o'-lanterns to the walls inside the kiosk. A record was playing on the portable Victrola he often brought down from his apartment, which was three floors above the kiosk in the same building. The cook owned a vast collection of tangos on old 78s featuring Argentina's legendary crooner, Carlos Gardel.

I opened the door to the stand and slipped into the alley beside Luigi. He had on a beautiful face mask that he must have made himself. His cheeks were unblemished and rosy, his forehead white as snow, his chin sweet and clean. I ordered a coffee and splurged on a pastelito. Roldán gave me a lollipop skull from Mexico for free. Luigi was already sucking on one.

Carlos the Artist came by wearing an atomic bomb costume fashioned from painted cardboard. Beside him Alfonso looked nutty in a beret, oversized vertigo spectacles, and a pair of plastic buckteeth. They carried shopping bags full of goodies obtained from trick-or-treating in Times Square.

"Eduardo was with us," Carlos said. He took off his nose cone, ordered a mate and a beef empanada, and snatched a lollipop skull from the box which was almost empty. His handlebar mustache was dyed bright red.

Alfonso removed his teeth and zany eyewear. He fetched his real glasses from a pocket and fitted them on carefully, blinking at us, focusing. Then he jumped back, startled, but only in jest. "Yikes, Luigi, you *scared* me."

"Eduardo can't stop bitching about Adriana," Carlos said. "He's going nuts over a woman he hates and isn't even married to anymore."

"Have a little sympathy, man." Alfonso quoted Pascal: "'The heart has its reasons which even reason does not understand.'"

Carlos said, "It's not his heart, it's the ego attached to his penis."

Alfonso said, "So what? I myself have a comparable dilemma. I'm torn between two women in Argentina who wish to be hitched to me. Renata is glamorous, passionate, and very unstable. I love her but she's crazy. Sofía is an even-keeled lady, a longtime friend whom I like but do not love. Yet I think it's her I will wind up with, much to my personal dismay."

Carlos scoffed, "That makes about as much sense as Eduardo's attitude toward Adriana."

"Not so fast, amigo." Alfonso dipped a wooden ice cream spoon into his little dulce de leche cup and licked off the caramel paste. "If I marry beautiful, tempestuous Renata, I am doomed. We'll end up in a loony bin together. But if I marry Sofía, I'll have a comfortable house and somebody to bring me my pipe and slippers. I'll eat well, live longer, and be a better mathematician. And eventually I'll forget Renata and learn to love Sofía."

I drummed up the courage to venture this opinion: "I think passion is more important than security."

Alfonso laughed and threw an arm around my shoulders. "Blondie, what could you possibly know about passion or security?"

Suddenly those boys had things to do and they disappeared, leaving me alone with Roldán. But before we could start a conversation a white limousine double-parked nearby and Chuy hopped out dressed in a red velvet devil suit. He ran to the kiosk, shouting, "Four chicken pies, chubby, and make it snappy! I've got three pibas in that meat wagon and we're late for a fiesta." He put a twenty on the window ledge. "Throw in four Cokes and straws and keep the change."

Chuy yanked a bunch of napkins from the aluminum dispenser and grabbed one of the Cokes Roldán had slapped onto the window ledge. "Help me, Hemingway, I've only got one hand," Chuy ordered. I picked up the other sodas and followed him to the limo.

Two of the girls wore full costumes; one was a tiger outfit, the other a black panther. The third girl was Cathy Escudero. She had on a flowery blue flamenco dress and no face mask. One hand held an open pink fan and she was smoking a cigarette.

"Apurate, manco," Cathy snapped at Chuy. "We can't be late. I do my number at midnight."

"Hold your water, kid, we'll get there."

I went back to the kiosk, wrapped three empanadas carefully in napkins, and carried them to the girls.

"Gracias," said the tiger, "muy amable."

"Te agradezco, Yankee," said the panther.

Cathy growled, "If this drips grease on my dress I'll strangle somebody."

Chuy hopped into the limo, shouted "Vámonos!" to the chauffeur, and they took off.

Roldán wiped his pudgy fingers on his apron and said, "That guy puts me in a black mood." He was huffing from exertion.

"Did you see the flamenco dancer?" I asked.

"How could I see her?" he grumbled. "I was cooking."

6. La Petisa

During the second week of November, Gino showed up for his night of work at the kiosk accompanied by a girl he introduced as his girlfriend, a half-pint ebullient chatterbox with dimples who wore slacks and a green Swiss hat with a badger brush in the band. Because she was small everyone called her La Petisa—which means "shorty."

"I'm a wanderer," she said. "I speak Spanish, French, English, and Italian, so you can see I have been around the block. My favorite, however, is French. I love Gino, of course, but his home is a pigsty."

Paying no attention to her, Gino prepared some empanadas for three elderly Italians smoking cigars while standing at the window: each of them wore a gray fedora.

"I do not understand how one who is as handsome as Gino could let his apartment become such a quilombo," La Petisa continued. "Look how well he dresses. Yet at home his clothes are lying everywhere, hanging over the radiators, slung under the bed, fallen off hangers onto the closet floor. The only furniture in his dump is a single mattress, no sheets, and the sink is always full of dirty dishes. The first thing I did when I arrived last week was buy a broom. I am going to whip that hellhole into shape."

"I'm going to whip *you* into shape if you don't shut up." Gino dropped three more beef and quince empanadas into the sizzling bin of fat.

"Hah." La Petisa jutted her tiny chin at him. "He who cannot even speak English is telling *moi* to *ferme ma gueule*? *Tu peux bien te taire toi-même*, Gino, *gros oeuf*."

Alfonso said, "Hey, that's impolite."

"Relax, the fool doesn't mind," she replied in English. "He can't understand French. Or English. He is completely vacant between the ears. But he's pretty, *n'est-ce pas*?"

Alfonso said, "What does it accomplish to speak one language or ten if you remain a barbarian in every lingo?"

"I'm not a barbarian, profe, I'm a lover."

"Then why do you talk crap to Gino in a foreign language when you know he only speaks Spanish?"

"It's a joke and he's a grown-up," La Petisa answered.

"No, it's not such a joke. To a kid it would be funny and he might understand. But adults are really sub-children and much too sensitive to absorb the mocking you give Gino."

"Oh hush, you're way too serious." La Petisa kissed Alfonso's cheek. "Truce, profe, I can't bear enemies. Please shake my hand."

They shook hands. Gino gave her a glower so she wouldn't kiss me, too. La Petisa said, "As soon as I get our crib cleaned up we'll have a big party with mate, empanadas, vino, and a parrilla. I'm a great chef. I can cook in five languages, you know."

"She can do something else in five languages, too." Gino winked at us as he set the dripping empanadas onto a paper towel on the window ledge for the Italians. They paid, bit off the pie tops, shook in Tabasco sauce, tipped their fedoras politely, and wandered north on MacDougal weaving calmly through the tourists.

Alfonso and I trailed after them. We àmbled past shabby trinket shops and Johnny's Italian Newsstand. In front of us a guy with a guitar entered the Gaslight to play for tips.

Standing under the Washington Square arch we gazed at the stormy sky for a minute. Leaves had fallen off all the trees.

"Dammit, friend, I'm horny," Alfonso admitted. "I envy Gino. I can't stand it that Renata and Sofía are so far away in Argentina. I wish I had a woman."

"Me too," I said bravely, thinking about Cathy Escudero.

A cold rain began to fall and pedestrians ran by shielding their heads with folded newspapers.

Alfonso groaned: "Qué soledad sin descanso!"

What a loneliness without end.

7. Apologies

Luigi couldn't bear it that Gino was screwing La Petisa.

Alfonso did not understand. "What's it to you?"

"She should be with me because I like her. I can't help it. If only she could see beyond my burnt face, I know that she'd love my soul."

"Gino's good-looking," Alfonso pointed out realistically. "He's big and strong. A natural magnet for women."

"I was more handsome than that dumb ox. He's a papier-mâché human being who is empty inside. I am the real thing. I read books, I go to movies, I can talk about Sartre and Miguel Ángel Asturias. I am a passionate and relevant man. Gino is a putz."

Alfonso draped an arm around Luigi's shoulders. "But you're short and you have a scary face. One day you'll land your woman, but she will be a rare specimen, and you'll have to watch out she doesn't bore you to death with compassion."

"No," Luigi said. "I want *this* one. Right *now.*"

"You can't have her," Alfonso said. "God doesn't hate you enough."

Popeye was growing bored with Luigi's rant. "Che, calm down, boludo. There's not a máquina on the globe that's worth blowing a gasket over."

Luigi spit at him.

Popeye looked down at the front of his shirt, horrified. Then he looked up at Luigi, who was looking at Popeye, appalled by what he'd done. Popeye looked over at Roldán, who shrugged and rolled his eyes. So the sailor man looked at me.

"Did you see *that*, blondie?"

Paralyzed, I did not know what to say.

Popeye appealed to Alfonso: "What did he do that for?"

"I don't know," the professor said. "Ask Luigi."

Popeye said, "Why did you do that, Luigi?"

"Because I'm an asshole," Luigi replied, thoroughly contrite. "I'll buy you a new shirt, marinero. I'm sorry. I apologize."

"It's okay," Popeye said. "I didn't mean to be so obnoxious, quemado. It was really my fault."

Luigi said, "No, no, *I'm* the guy who is ashamed and needs to make amends. I lost control. There's no excuse . . ."

Alfonso hoisted an imaginary violin and began to play it.

8. A Desperate Request

I typed all morning and half the afternoon on Thanksgiving, then went for a walk up West Broadway. It was a cold, windy day beneath an overcast sky. On Bleecker Street I turned left and headed past the Village Gate and the Greenwich Hotel, a flophouse. The empanada stand was closed and Roldán had taped an announcement in Spanish to the plywood window shutter:

> DAY OF THANKS
> Come upstairs if you are hungry.
> There is safety in numbers.

I climbed three flights to his door and knocked loudly. Presently the fat man opened up, saying, "Bienvenido, blondie. Mi casa es tu casa."

He wore a filthy T-shirt, baggy boxer shorts, old blue flip-flops. The apartment was very hot; I began perspiring like an empanada in the grease bin. I followed him to the kitchen where an enormous turkey sat on a platter on the table. He indicated a chair for me and settled down on the other side with the bird between us. There was an open bottle of wine and he poured me some.

"Take whatever meat you need, muchacho. It's a big bird. Want me to cut a chunk for you?"

"No. I can handle it." Being alone with Roldán made me uncomfortable. His TV was tuned to a football game.

"Have any of the patota been by?" I asked.

"No, nobody from the gang. They're all out eating with Pilgrims who intend to shoot them later on." He chuckled.

I felt tongue-tied. Roldán was vaguely soused and had a slight lisp. His clothes were soaked through with sweat. Huge droplets of salty moisture had gathered across his forehead, creating rivulets down to his cheeks. I filled my plate with turkey and stuffing, cranberry sauce, a sweet potato. Then I raised my glass in a toast:

"Salud, amor, dinero—"

"—y muchisimo tiempo para gastarlos."

Health, love, money . . . and all the time in the world to spend them.

The cook proffered his own glass with awkward gusto, slopping out a few drops. Then we consumed food quietly until he asked me, "Why aren't you eating with your family?"

"They live far away in California."

I asked him about his own family.

"My mother died when I was three. My father shot himself with an antique firearm. I lived with my grandmother until she tossed me out. They are all dead and buried, rest in peace."

"Do you have brothers and sisters?"

"Eleven. We split up early. Seven of us survived, but I lost track when I was still very young. You know, during the Depression."

When I inquired, "Have you ever been married?" Roldán laughed, saying, "Good God, no." Yet he dug into a back pocket for his wallet, removing from it a tattered arcade photograph rubbed almost illegible. He handed it over to me. I could barely make out a youngster with an angelic face framed by curly blonde hair.

"A long time ago I fell in love with that girl. We lived in my room at a boardinghouse for six months. Then she left and never returned."

He reached for the picture and I gave it back to him. "If she had stuck around I would have married her."

"Why did she leave?"

"I don't know." He studied the picture thoughtfully. "We screwed each other like babies and she cuddled every night in my arms. She could fall asleep in ten seconds, and I watched her snooze for hours completely relaxed like a puppy."

"After she left did you receive any letters?"

He shook his head. "She was illiterate. I remember that her hands were smaller than mice and very quick. She could pinch flies off the windowpane between her thumb and forefinger."

"What was her name?" I asked.

"Teresa Mono." He made a small gesture of dismissal and put away her photograph. He had trouble stuffing the chunky wallet back into his rear pocket. Then he said, "When she left me my heart was broken and I ran away from Argentina for consolation."

Roldán had worked in Bolivian coal mines. He started a restaurant in Lima, Peru, that was successful until he offended the gangsters who made his liquor deliveries. In Nicaragua he repaired tractors and other large machinery on a finca near the ocean. Then came Guatemala. There he owned a street cart from which he sold popcorn, potato chips, peanuts, and soda pop. The refrain he cried out all day long, every day for three years, was: "Poporopo, papalina, maní y agua!"

The cocinero opened his first empanada stand in Mexico

City. It kept him afloat for two years until he grew bored and purchased a bus ticket to New York.

I said, "You've been to a lot of countries. You've witnessed many things, Roldán."

"Yes, I've seen a lot of shit, blondie." He hefted another sweet potato, devouring it like an empanada. "Our planet is a truly remarkable pigpen. I have seen children with their throats slit in the gutter, and a man with a machine gun preparing to kill a woman. On a Nicaragua beach I saw a dead shark twice the size of a car. The Lima homeless sleep on cold streets in beds of piss, but there is a library more fabulous than a cathedral. More turkey?"

"No, gracias." I looked at my watch and got up to leave. I had to wash dishes at the Night Owl. Roldán shook my hand, telling me to go with God. I thanked him for the meal and for the stories. At the door he said, "Maybe I'll see you tomorrow night at the empanada stand?"

"Maybe," I said, and then I blurted, "Listen, I'd like to meet one of the girls in Chuy's book but I don't know how to arrange it."

He said, "It's simple. Ask Chuy when next you see him."

"Tengo vergüenza." I felt ashamed.

"Do you want me to ask him for you?"

I nodded my head desperately, *yes,* and hurried down the stairs.

Outside, a few flakes of dry snow were swirling and it had almost gotten dark. I scurried up MacDougal Street with my head bowed against the wind, gasping in big gulps of icy air. I felt as if I had jumped out of an airplane and pulled my rip cord, but I did not know if the parachute would open.

9. Cathy Escudero

When I met Chuy under the Washington Square arch it was snowing lightly. The big Christmas tree displayed hundreds of shining lights. A bum wearing a Santa Claus outfit stood beside a Salvation Army kettle ringing his bell monotonously. Fifth Avenue buses coughed out black fumes at busy shoppers who hurried back and forth around us.

Chuy said, "Come on, we'll catch a cab."

I had never been rich enough to hail a taxi in New York. It carried us up to Fourteenth Street, then west to the corner of Eighth Avenue. Chuy gave the driver a one-dollar tip. We entered a dilapidated building located mid-block and rode a ramshackle elevator to the fourth floor. Chuy said, "It's rare for an Argentine to dance flamenco. But this girl is a true disciple." Way down the corridor he opened a thick metal door and we stepped into a bare room lined by mirrors and with ballet barres about waist high along one wall. Seated against the far windows was a skinny young man in a thin coat and scarf and porkpie hat playing a guitar. The coils of a small electric heater glowed red at his feet.

Cathy Escudero wore a black practice skirt and flamenco shoes and a baggy T-shirt knotted at her navel. Her dark hair was pulled back in a bun. She was barely five feet tall but the clatter of her shoes sounded like thunder. Chuy patted my shoulder, wished me, "Suerte, nene," and disappeared.

I sat down against the east wall, clasped my knees, and let out a quiet sigh. I could see my breath on the cold air. Neither guitarist nor dancer acknowledged me. They were concentrating on the music and the footwork.

Cathy moved abruptly, hard and choppy, with fanatical precision one second and then with a delicate and sinuous counterpoint the next. Her style was graceful but shocking. The guy played his guitar like hammer blows, then shifted into a poignant ripple. He and Cathy started and stopped in unison. The dance seemed angry and sexual and very fast. Some of Cathy's hair shook loose and strands were pasted against her damp cheeks. She spun and stomped and built to a crescendo. The guitarist watched her every move like a fanatic planning an assassination. He was good, a Spaniard it turned out, and no older than seventeen.

They ended with a sudden crash. I wanted to clap but resisted the impulse. Panting, Cathy said, "I fucked up the second llamada. I always fuck it up. I *hate* fucking it up."

She went to her purse on the floor and retrieved a pack of cigarettes. She gave one to the guitarist and called over to me, "Querés un faso?"

"No, gracias."

Cathy leaned against a mirror, smoking, sweating heavily. In Spanish she told me, "My name is Cathy and this is Jorge. We're both going to be famous. What do you do for a living?"

I explained that I was trying to be a writer, but meanwhile I washed dishes at the Night Owl Café and unloaded trucks for the Houston Street Labor Pool.

"I want to be rich," she said. "My father is a janitor. I work at El Parrillón, a restaurant uptown on Forty-seventh Street. My mother sews cheap sweatshop dresses. They can't even speak English. Before two years are over I swear that I'm going to be a star. I'm not a gypsy, but that doesn't matter. I pity anyone who gets in my way."

When she finished the cigarette Cathy dropped it on the floor and crushed it under her shoe.

"Let's do alegrías," she said to Jorge.

He struck a hard, short note. She twisted into a lovely anguished shape—ready. Then they began.

I sat quietly for an hour, enthralled and impervious to the cold. They repeated every move and each note a hundred times. They stopped, went back, tried once more. They went over and over it again until a troupe of diminutive pixies in ballet costumes chaperoned by an adult carrying a small Victrola and a bag of records took over the studio. I walked downstairs with Jorge and Cathy Escudero.

On the sidewalk the girl shook my hand good-bye. "Come by whenever you want," she said. "We practice three times a week at this hour. I like an audience. It gives me an edge."

10. Carlos the Artist

Carlos the Artist often wore a cape, a black jersey, black pants, and black boots with elevated heels. He also worshiped Marcel Duchamp and the film *Last Year at Marienbad*. His paintings were surreal but good. He was slated for a show at an uptown cultural center next spring.

Meanwhile, Carlos had been married three times and never officially divorced. Now he had a problem because his present wife did not work and remained at home all day long while Carlos tried to paint. She distracted him and they spent a lot of hours in bed. The artist sat around drinking and moping and complaining to her that he couldn't make his art. Eventually—desperately—he approached me.

"Oíme. Don't give me any guff. I need an apartment tomorrow between three and three-thirty. Can I have your key?"

"Why for only half an hour?"

He shrugged. "That makes it more exciting."

"All right. I'll drop off an extra key with Roldán after I finish my stint at the Night Owl. You can come by and pick it up when you need it. Be careful not to kick the manuscripts stacked across my floor."

"You have a friend for life, blondie. My house will always be your house."

The next day when I was due out of the apartment, Alfonso and I saw Francois Truffaut's movie *Jules and Jim*. The mathematics professor was a movie buff and together we had already seen *Breathless, Viridiana,* and *La Dolce Vita; also Black Orpheus, Rashomon,* and *La Strada.* Alfonso knew the schedules at museums or out-of-the-way art theaters, and we usually attended screenings in the mornings or early after-noons—whenever the price was cheapest.

When we emerged from *Jules and Jim* I felt confused and excited. I was enthralled by Jeanne Moreau and identified with Jules, the timid Oskar Werner character. The mood of that story about two men obsessed with the same woman made me uncomfortable. I knew I had witnessed wonderful secrets impossible to understand that were nevertheless integral to human relationships and tinged by enormous sorrow.

Alfonso and I wandered around for a spell discussing the movie. We circled the Washington Square fountain a half dozen times and then watched some bearded guys moving their pawns and bishops at the southwest corner chess tables. Alfonso had on his thin yellow sarape and a shaggy purple scarf. It was sunny but cold.

"Jeanne Moreau reminds me of my girlfriend Renata," Alfonso said. "Yesterday I received another letter from her, the second this week. Five pages long. Threatening to enter a convent if we don't get married soon. She sent a picture of herself in a bathing suit." He paused. "My other girl, Sofía, is like Jules—she's patient, she's deferential, she's understanding. Sometimes I despise her for that."

"I would fall in love with Jeanne Moreau," I said. "I wouldn't care what happened."

"Yes you would," Alfonso said, patting my back. "Let's go to Figaro's for a peek at their cute new waitress."

We walked down Thompson Street, turned right on Bleecker, and stopped at the coffeehouse. The windows were blurry with condensation. We found a cleared area and peered inside at cozy people nursing hot chocolates while playing chess.

Alfonso pointed. "There she is. The little blonde one. She speaks with a strange accent, I think from Boston. I wouldn't mind screwing her just to get my rocks off."

I said, "Speaking of that, right now while we're standing in the cold, Carlos the Artist is using my apartment to take out his frustrations on some poor waif while his wife probably sits at home ignorant of the whole affair."

Alfonso couldn't care less. "In her letter Renata described ten ways she plans to have sex with me. She's highly inspired in bed. Of course, it's a trap. Though by comparison, making love with Sofía is like eating a lukewarm bowl of soup or reading Proust."

Somebody tapped my shoulder. It was Carlos with a sexy plump girl on his arm. Fifteen minutes ago she had been wearing red lipstick that was now smeared all over the painter's five o'clock shadow. Carlos slipped me my apartment key, winked, and whispered, "A thousand thanks, amigo." Then he and the girl stepped over a bum and sauntered off arm in arm, pleasantly exhausted.

"I feel sorry for his wife," I said. "It's a rotten thing to do."

"That *is* his wife," Alfonso said, adjusting his purple scarf with an energetic flourish.

11. Ambition

"Oh my, you're back already?" Cathy's eyes had a suspicious look. "It must be the perfume I'm wearing. Welcome to our humble studio. Please don't clap or throw me plata until the performance is over, okay?"

"Okay." I sat on the floor far from them and wrapped my arms around my knees.

Cathy said, "Do you know anything about flamenco, blondie?"

I shook my head. "No."

Jorge reached one hand down to warm up at the heater beside his feet, then he extended the other hand. He was wearing his porkpie hat.

"It's not something I'm going to explain," Cathy said. "You just have to watch us and learn for yourself. Okay?"

"Okay," I said again.

Raising her hands, she fiddled with her hair, tucking loose strands back into the bun. Out of boredom Jorge played a fast little riff that he would not have included while Cathy danced.

She said, "And just so it's clear, Chuy's a friend of mine but I would never screw him, do you understand?"

I nodded my head. "Yes."

"He has a lot of money, and sometimes he helps people. Who knows why, but there's not a string attached. Some bastards are also sentimental if you play your cards right."

I nodded some more, like one of those dipper birds on the side of a water glass.

Cathy spoke to Jorge so fast I didn't catch a word. He immediately started playing a tune that I later learned was a

Sevillana. Cathy liked to warm up with Sevillanas, simple folk dances that usually two women do together. Sevillanas have a brief introduction, followed by three short repeated stanzas, and a sudden finish. They all follow a similar pattern, requiring no great dexterity. Flamenco is very mathematical and for beginners there is not room for improvisation. Every move and every stroke must be learned by heart, requiring absolute precision.

When Cathy was ready they became serious. They talked to each other and Jorge played in slow motion while she worked something out. They speeded up a little, and then they went even faster. Cathy grabbed the sides of her skirt and swished it, she gritted her teeth and frowned, concentrating furiously, and Jorge never took his eyes off her. To make it work they had to be in sync. Sometimes Cathy shouted "Otra vez!" right in the middle, and Jorge jumped back to the beginning without a hitch.

I had never seen people working so hard to be artists.

"Maybe when you publish your first book you'll dedicate it to me," Cathy said afterward, gasping as she pulled on some dungarees, then stripped her skirt off down and over them. "Do you think you will ever publish a book?"

I shrugged, smiling self-consciously. "I don't know."

"If you *don't know* you're fucked," she said. "I *know* I'm going to succeed, not just in Argentina or New York, but one day also in Spain. It's a fact, written in my blood."

And abruptly they left the studio.

12. Shaken

Walking home after that dance session I was shaken. My tenement stood four blocks south of Washington Square on the corner of West Broadway and Prince Street. The apartment cost $42.50 a month. As I climbed up to the fifth floor I thought: Nobody ever publishes a book unless they submit it to a publisher. But I was still afraid to do that.

I sat in my wooden chair and stared at stacks of typing paper covering the floor. They comprised various drafts of my novels, also carbon copies of short stories that I sent out regularly. There was a pile of journals I had kept since high school. I did not own a filing cabinet. All told I had twenty different piles on the floor.

I was obsessed. And I was in a hurry because I didn't know if, or when, I would be drafted. Though the world situation was tense, I completely avoided news about the Cold War heating up. I just wanted to be a writer.

One novel followed the last week on earth of an alcoholic Bowery bum. Another I considered my Scott Fitzgerald story, about the collapse of a Long Island robber baron family. My Carson McCullers tale unfolded in a small Vermont town during World War II. My college romance novel was almost slapstick and featured an outrageous female narrator.

I typed at a cheap metal table painted to resemble wood. My machine was a small green Hermes Rocket that had cost forty dollars. I owned no TV or telephone or sheets for the tin bed that had come with the place when I rented it. My covers were an old army surplus sleeping bag.

My paperback books occupied shelves beside the bed: Faulkner, Hemingway, Thomas Wolfe. Every week I bought a couple more novels secondhand for a quarter each from stores over on Fourth Avenue below Union Square. If I wasn't writing I immersed myself in literature. I really *studied* fiction, hoping to absorb its secrets.

Yet how did you even approach a publisher?

Picking up manuscripts, I riffled through them. Most had been started in school. The Vermont novel was in its third rewrite and still pretty rough. My robber baron epic was in its second rewrite, but too self-conscious. The Bowery bum tale lacked a complete first draft. However, the college romance had been through five incarnations and it was my favorite. Less ambitious than the others, but more complete.

Slowly, I scanned that book, whispering sentences aloud. I reread the last fifteen pages, which left me cold. How could this be? Nervously, I changed some punctuation and made other corrections. I wondered: How could you work so hard on a book and yet remain ambivalent?

Then I decided to rewrite the college romance one more time, and after that I would attempt to get it published.

13. Death of a Crooner

My Argentine pals could not resist the lure of Rockefeller Center during the holiday season. Alfonso, Luigi, and I took a bus up there and walked around for an afternoon. We bumped into Eduardo, who tagged along with us as we ogled the enormous decorated tree and the gold statue of Prometheus. We gazed at rich people skating circles at the ice rink. In St. Patrick's Cathedral, Luigi and Eduardo lit several candles.

"Who are you lighting them for?" Alfonso asked.

"I am lighting this candle for my own face," Luigi answered.

Eduardo said, "I am lighting this candle so God will strike down my wife, Adriana, with a thunderbolt."

"She's not your wife, she's your ex-wife," Luigi reminded him.

Alfonso lit one taper for Renata, his volatile Argentine lover, and another for Sofía, his pragmatic Buenos Aires girlfriend.

"I'm playing it safe," he explained. "Like Henry the Eighth."

We mingled with the crowds and ate hot chestnuts and bought four green cookies shaped like evergreen trees. Bells rang, carols played, and everyone had rosy cheeks. Alfonso showed us the building where Diego Rivera had done a mural that the Rockefellers destroyed because it depicted the face of Lenin. Eduardo complained that he hadn't been laid ever since Adriana began dating the "pimp."

We went window-shopping up one side of Fifth Avenue to the Plaza Hotel at Fifty-ninth Street and down the other side toward Forty-second Street. Cheery colored lights blinked around displays of jewelry on beds of angel hair. I wanted to buy Cathy Escudero a Christmas present. I wanted to spend all the dollars I could earn over a year for a gold bracelet, a string of pearls, or a pair of diamond earrings from Tiffany's or Van Cleef & Arpels.

Instead, Eduardo borrowed ten bucks from me. "I'm broke. I forgot my wallet." That cleaned me out. "Don't worry, blondie, I'll give it back when next we meet at the kiosk."

Luigi halted dead in his tracks. A beautiful woman was approaching us, tall and brunette, wearing silver hoop earrings and a knee-length mink coat. Her hair bounced against her shoulders with great verve and she had an air of self-satisfied gaiety. She carried no packages so her arms were swinging freely.

The burnt man spread his hands wide apart and, in heavily accented English, proclaimed to the universe, "Look at this beautiful woman!"

The lady stopped, contemplating our comrade with a perplexed frown. Then she brightened, laughing. "And you are a beautiful guy." She walked right up to Luigi, kissed him on the cheek—"Merry Christmas, little man"—and continued on her way.

"What about *me*?" Eduardo called after her in Spanish. To us he moaned, "You see? Adriana has cursed me. When we were married I had a dozen chicas on the side. Now that I'm 'free' they ignore me because I'm a cuckold."

When we reached Forty-second Street Alfonso said, "Let's go into the library."

We crossed the avenue. Two small boys were sitting astride one of the concrete lions while their father took a picture. Inside, Alfonso led us upstairs to the newspaper reading room. He checked out a *New York Times* microfilm and we gathered around him while he searched for the day that Argentina's famous singer Carlos Gardel had died—Monday, June 24, 1935.

An article explained that after a successful Bogotá concert, Gardel's plane had taken off for Cali, via Medellín. The plane was a Ford tri-motor F-31 belonging to SACO, a Colombian airline. After refueling at Olaya Herrera airport in Medellín, the plane taxied onto the runway and collided with another aircraft, bursting into flame. Seventeen passengers died, five were miraculously saved. Burned beyond recognition, Gardel's body was identified through an ID bracelet and dental records. He was seated next to the pilot and probably expired instantly. His band members, his secretary, and his masseur also perished. His English professor survived.

We emerged from the library at dusk, riding the subway downtown to Astor Place. Over at the empanada stand Roldán had the sliding glass window partially open. A clump of mistletoe was tacked to the overhead frame above a string of flashing lights. His portable Victrola on the ledge was playing a record of Elvis Presley singing Christmas tunes. Gino and Popeye were lounging on the sidewalk smoking cigarettes and eyeing three NYU girls also listening to the music while they sipped coffee and sucked on Hershey Kisses from a basket Roldán kept on the window ledge. Gino had on a new Borsalino hat. Alfonso asked to replace Elvis with Carlos

Gardel and the fat man obliged. Luigi chose the record, a scratched 78 that gave out a lot of static. The coeds trotted away. Collars up, shoulders hunched, hands thrust deeply into our pockets, we boys huddled together in a semicircle on the sidewalk listening to these words in Spanish:

> The clown, with all his funny faces
> and exaggerated smiles,
> is inviting us, dear friends,
> to enjoy the carnival.
> You can't see by his smile
> all the pain that's underneath;
> his face of frozen cheerfulness
> hides the awful truth.

While we listened to this song, Luigi's deformed features assumed a disturbing radiance. Pedestrians wandered by carrying bags of gift-wrapped presents. Soon it began to snow and the storm did not stop for two days.

14. Moth to a Flame

I woke up at three P.M. with an icing of white stuff on the window ledges. The fire escape outside my kitchen was frosted by dazzling meringue. I kneeled beside a clanking radiator and inhaled the warm bread odor from Vesuvio's bakery. Thick snow was still falling and a premature darkness muffled the tenements. No trucks were unloading on West Broadway. A single pedestrian under a red umbrella scuffed along the center of the street. Two chairs outside the Sons of Italy Social Club had fluff piled five inches high. While I was sleeping the city had come to a standstill.

I bundled up and hurried downstairs feeling buoyant and excited. I was due at the Night Owl at four. New York stifled by the storm was amazing. The lack of noise was eerie. I crossed Houston, prancing through unsullied snow that rose well above my ankles.

The café had a CLOSED BECAUSE OF WEATHER sign on the door. So I kept going. Only a few sets of tracks crisscrossed the open areas of Washington Square. The Christmas tree under the arch was lit up and beautiful. No commerce plied Fifth Avenue where the awnings of fancy apartment buildings sagged beneath the weight of snow. A woman kept snug by luxurious fur stood uncomfortably with her arms folded while her Pomeranian shivered in a drift.

I walked north pummeled gently by the insistent flakes. Traffic lights blinked from green to yellow to red and back again, but there was nobody to be directed across the intersections. Visibility was only a few blocks.

I didn't know I was headed for the dance studio until I arrived. On Fourteenth Street, halfway between Eighth and Ninth avenues, I heard Jorge's guitar. They had a window open. When I showed up they were hard at work as if nothing unusual had submerged the city's clamor. I arranged myself in a corner creating a puddle around me on the floor.

Snow falling was reflected in the studio mirrors, which cast shadows over us like sunshine rippling underwater. Jorge played a slow tune and Cathy stretched languidly while bending into the dolorous shapes of her craft. Jorge's fingers released pensive notes I had never heard. The guitarist and the dancer cast a delicate spell with their remarkable balancing act.

Cathy went through a series of small hesitations; she inclined forward like a grieving widow, compassionate and tragic.

Jorge stopped. Cathy was left hanging as he put aside his guitar; then his partner sank to the floor. They sat quietly, luxuriating in torpor. The one to break it was Jorge when he reached for a cigarette. Cathy said, "Dame un pitillo."

She lit it herself and exhaled deeply. A defiant shadow tweaked her features. They smoked in silence until Cathy asked me, "How did you get here?"

"I walked."

"Vos sos loco."

"Yes I am."

She replied, "Did you publish a novel yet?"

That startled me.

"No . . . not yet."

Her shoulders sagged and she picked discontentedly at a blemish on the floor.

"How did *you* guys get here?" I asked.

When she glanced up at me Cathy's eyes had a provocative twinkle.

"We paid for a limousine."

On Fourteenth Street in the dark I wanted to shove her playfully and instigate a snowball fight, but Jorge tromped seriously ahead of us in measured rhythm like an ascetic holy man. Street lamps were dimmed by the storm: Flakes wiggled like twirling cells breeding under a microscope. Cathy hugged the heavy dance bag to her chest and hunched her shoulders.

Jorge strode down into the subway entrance. Cathy paused on the threshold looking up at me. Her charming disconsolate face was ashen, her teeth chattered.

"Adiós, gringito," she said.

"Adiós, Cathy."

Then she pattered down the steps, hurrying to catch up with Jorge while I waved good-bye like somebody in a movie.

15. Spaghetti for Jesus

On the afternoon of Christmas Eve La Petisa said, "Luigi's apartment is like no place I have ever seen before. It is the haunt of a lunatic, the product of a mind as burnt as his face."

"What do you know about Luigi's apartment? You visited there with Gino?"

We had met by chance on Bleecker Street and entered the Café Borgia for tea. The room was full to the brim with pink-cheeked last-minute shoppers. Outside, wind blew fresh snowdrifts down MacDougal and across Bleecker. I was happy because my college romance novel was going great but I was afraid to discuss it with anyone.

La Petisa said, "Gino is too much of a slob for me. I would get everything neat one minute, but next minute he would mess it up again. After one of our fights he tore all my clothes out of the closet and threw them onto the kitchen floor. Al final fue una joda despelote. Every time I put the toilet paper in correctly, he flipped it backwards. Then Gino threw me out and Luigi took me in. Of course, to sleep we use separate beds: It's a platonic relationship. His place is warmer than Gino's, but there's a Buddhist altar and dozens of vulgar magazines on the bookshelves. In the bathroom are barbells that Luigi never uses. However, once a day a strange beast with a beard and hair down to its shoulders appears and spends fifteen minutes working out with the barbells. The beast is Luigi's friend El Coco. And that guy *really* bugs me."

Looking up I saw Roldán's nose pressed against the window and waved to get his attention. He walked around to the door and limped in. He was wearing an old raccoon coat, a knitted cap, and his face was half hidden by a woolen scarf. He sat down, unwound the scarf, unbuttoned his coat, and lit a cigar he'd just purchased at Johnny's Italian Newsstand.

"Qué carajo invierno!" he exclaimed. "I never experienced this in Argentina or Bolivia or Mexico City."

La Petisa patted his hand. "Listen, tomorrow everybody's meeting at Fugazzi for dinner, correct?"

"De acuerdo." Fugazzi was a small Italian restaurant on Sixth Avenue a block west of the empanada stand. "I made reservations for fifteen."

"But should we really have an Italian dinner on Christmas?" La Petisa made a wry face. "I mean, what way is that to celebrate the birth of Jesus?"

"A ravioli or a goose, what's the difference?" Roldán shook salt onto his large palm and licked it. "I wouldn't be surprised if Joseph and Mary sat down to a good spaghetti dinner after Jesus was safely asleep in the manger."

Alfonso came over to our table stomping snow off his shoes.

"It was scampi," he announced, unwinding his purple scarf. "I'm sure they had scampi or veal cacciatore that day. Maybe osso buco." He took off a ridiculous red-and-yellow cap with earflaps and a bell at the tip. "Christ it's cold outside."

He also removed an elegant pair of fur-lined leather gloves and slapped them onto the table.

La Petisa warned the professor: "Don't be blasphemous. God hears everything."

"Oh? And what does He think about you who goes to bed with Gino out of wedlock?" Alfonso called the waitress over, ordering an espresso.

La Petisa said, "Hey, I'm a good Catholic. I go to Mass every Sunday. For two years after my father died I wore a black armband and went to the cathedral each morning to light a candle. And I'm living with Luigi now, since Gino threw me out." She added: "Where did you get that woeful hat?"

"It's a Christmas present from my novia Renata in Buenos Aires."

"Her taste is in her ass."

"Oi." Alfonso arched way back. "She's got a lot more imagination than *you* do, shorty."

"What about the gloves, profe? Same piba? At least they look useful."

"They're a gift from Sofía." Alfonso tugged the gloves back on approvingly and flexed the fingers. "My other novia, the sensible one."

"Marry the gloves," La Petisa advised. "If you marry that hat you're a dead man."

16. Eskimos

What a snowstorm! Roldán did not have a Christmas tree so we decided to buy him one. Two blocks south on Sullivan Street we located a few ratty shrubs corralled inside a wooden fence. A boy wearing an Aztec ski mask ran out of a bar to make the deal with us, then hurried back inside.

We carried the tree home to Roldán's apartment three floors above the empanada stand. La Petisa left to search for ornaments while Alfonso and the boss mixed hot rum toddies in a blender. We listened to a record by Edith Piaf. La Petisa returned twenty minutes later with colored paper, glue, gold paint, and Luigi, who was wearing a white Santa Claus beard full of snow. We clicked on the TV to a Perry Como Christmas special. I cut out snowflakes; La Petisa made bells and angels from the colored paper. Alfonso and Luigi fashioned elaborate paper cockroaches. There was a brief argument about the cockroaches. We snipped a tin coffee lid into the shape of a star for the treetop.

Eduardo dropped by with a bottle of wine. He was already drunk because he'd seen Adriana and her fat "pimp" getting out of a taxi that afternoon. We ignored him. Eduardo never mentioned the ten dollars he owed me. Gino and Chuy also appeared and hugged everybody except Luigi, who almost snarled at Gino when Gino embraced La Petisa. The newcomers were all eager to share dinner with us tomorrow at Fugazzi. Chuy had a bag with two magnums of French champagne in it. We drank them, then bundled up and stumbled outside to sing carols. Snow was falling harder. As we walked up the middle of MacDougal Street old people leaned from their windows listening to our voices belting out holiday ballads in Spanish. A snowball landed on Luigi's head; another one knocked off Gino's new Borsalino. In retaliation we bombarded a third-floor window with snowballs.

"Feliz Navidad!" Luigi yelled up at the windows.

We tramped north on MacDougal, kicking apart clouds of white stuff. Eduardo cried, "I hate her! She's a witch!" La Petisa said, "Oh grow up, you baby." At West Fourth Street we turned into Washington Square and wandered around the park and through the arch onto Fifth Avenue and up to Eighth Street and back again. Chuy told Eduardo, "Forget her. I'll find you a better one." We continued down Sullivan Street to St. Anthony's Church on the southeast corner across Houston. All the church lights were on and the crèche figures were covered by snow. The sheep had thick powdery fleeces. Joseph had a white cone on his head. A loudspeaker played "O Little Town of Bethlehem," drowning out our voices, so we shut up and listened, huddling for warmth and stamping our feet alongside a dozen other Eskimos enjoying the show.

Eduardo said, "I don't *want* any of your girls, manco. I can seduce women by myself. Get away from me. You're giving me escalofríos."

"Pipe down, all of you," Alfonso ordered.

Chuy shouted, "Oh my God—I almost forgot!" And he ran away through the storm, late for an important date.

"We can't come to the dinner at Fugazzi," La Petisa admitted. "Tomorrow we're dining with friends of the family in Queens. In fact, we should go now, Luigi. We'll need plenty of sleep to deal with them."

Luigi balked. "I detest those self-righteous prigs. I'm staying right here with my pals so we can eat together mañana."

La Petisa walked off in a huff. Gino said, "I'll go with her," and he did.

"Tu puta madre!" Luigi called after him.

We traipsed east for another block and turned right, down to Milady's Bar on the corner of Prince and Thompson Streets, one block west of my tenement. Alfonso, Luigi, and I played pool while Roldán and Eduardo talked with two college girls from Greenwich, Connecticut. The pool table was small and each rack cost a quarter. In a corner booth some happy drunken yokels sang "Silent Night," the Italian version. At ten Eduardo departed with both the minas and the cook appeared at the pool table. By eleven, feeling sick from all the smoke, we left Milady's and bought bagels and cream cheese at Miguel's All-Nite Puerto Rican Deli on Spring Street. Church bells were calling people to midnight Mass.

Back at Roldán's apartment there was no leftover wine to drink and Luigi grew pensive. "I don't mean to sound like a spoilsport, but that girl is all alone. I can't leave her like that."

"She went with Gino," Roldán reminded him.

"That's worse than being alone." Luigi added, "She refuses to make love with me, but damned if I'll let her bring that good-looking asshole to my place."

So he bid us adieu. That left Alfonso, me, and Roldán. The cook toasted our bagels and slathered on the cream cheese, and then added sardines and pickle slices. He and Alfonso were drunk. When Eduardo banged on the door we let him in. We brushed snow off his head and shoulders. "They laughed at me," he whined. "They told me to 'drop dead.'

Nobody tells me to 'drop dead.' Look at me, I'm a man. *I am a man.*"

Alfonso looked at him. "No you aren't," he said. "All I see is a jealous, paranoid hypochondriac."

That befuddled Eduardo. "What are you talking about, you fucker? What are you *talking* about?"

Roldán said, "Easy, boys. Let's not get personal here."

"What do *you* think, blondie?" Alfonso asked. "We need a neutral opinion."

"What do I think about *what*?" I stammered.

When we awoke many hours later, all four of us joined up again and tromped through brilliant sunshine and snowy streets to Fugazzi for a lavish meal of spaghetti with clam sauce and Chianti wine. Three small tables were shoved together to accommodate us plus La Petisa, Luigi, Popeye, Gino, Carlos the Artist and his wife, El Coco, and Chuy and his accountant, Greta Garbo, all of whom had promised to join us. But none of them showed up. Caruso played during the meal. The waiter was an old Italian who could speak Spanish because he'd fought with an International Brigade during the civil war. He sat down beside us at the end to smoke cigars provided by Eduardo.

We raised our wineglasses.

And Roldán paid for everything.

17. Santa, Baby

The day after Christmas I went to the dance studio where Cathy Escudero and Jorge were hard at work, same as before. I pushed open the door slowly. Cathy stopped right in the middle of her dance and snapped, "Dale, gringo, either come in or go out, but don't just stand there."

I hustled to the far wall and sat down with my shoulders hunched, as inconspicuous as possible.

Cathy called over, "What did Santa Claus bring you for Christmas?"

I shook my head, embarrassed—nothing at all.

"He brought me a fur coat, silk stockings, and a satin garter belt," she said, grabbing a pack of cigarettes off the windowsill. "You want to see them?"

I cocked my head, staring at her quizzically.

The dancer lit her cigarette, then turned around, bent over, and swished up her skirt, mooning me. There were no stockings and no garter belt, only her white cotton panties and pretty legs.

It lasted only a second before she laughed, dropping the skirt and facing me.

"You know what Santa Claus brought Jorge?" she asked.

By now I was confused and at her mercy.

"He brought Jorge a big lump of coal and the rent bill," she said, blowing smoke out her nose. "Christmas in America is crazy. Okay, muchacho, hit it."

Jorge started again at exactly the spot where I had interrupted. Cathy grabbed her skirt and began to pound the floor with the incongruous cigarette still in her mouth. She danced that way for five minutes with the weed between her lips like a tough little Humphrey Bogart. It never disturbed her concentration. A few times she inhaled and then exhaled smoke in huffing bursts, but she never touched the cigarette with her fingers. When it had burned down almost to a nub she spit it out and gasped loudly and finished the dance. The nub burned out on the floor.

Cathy panted, dripping with sweat. She pulled up the hem of her skirt, tucking it into the waistband, exposing her legs from the knees down.

She said, "In Argentina the Three Wise Men place candy in our shoes on January sixth, the day of Los Reyes. Little kids put their wish lists outside the door by their zapatos. They also leave some hay and a bowl of water for the camels. But my family never had money for presents. In fact, if any of us had ever seen Rudolph the Red-Nosed Reindeer we would have slit his throat and turned him into sausage on a parrilla. Here's a nice memory, though. When the Peronistas still held power they brought trucks to the barrio full of toys and gave them to us poor kids. One year I got a ball and a yo-yo and a notebook. That's the last time I ever received something for nothing. In real life if you want anything good you have to kill yourself to grasp it. Isn't that right, Jorge?"

Jorge shrugged and smoked his cigarette like a professional actor in a gangster movie. To me, the two of them together seemed like ancient souls trapped in adolescent bodies. And for the rest of that practice session they ignored me completely.

18. Big Tits, Blue Hair

On New Year's Eve I quit typing on my college romance at nine P.M. Then I walked up to the empanada stand where the cocinero was cutting cards for nickels with Gino and Carlos the Artist while he cooked. The boys squeezed over to let me in the alley. Their tattered deck of cards featured sleazy naked ladies. I put four nickels on the counter and joined the game. The great Gardel was singing his laments on the Victrola. Three inches of wet snow covered the sidewalk and it was still falling like blobs of frozen custard. Despite the cold, revelers were all over the place. Taxicabs honked loudly in the traffic jams on Bleecker and MacDougal.

"What's your New Year's resolution, blondie?" Roldán scooped up three nickels for producing the queen of spades, a bosomy gal with her lips puckered in a kiss. The cook poured each of us a shot of wine from a bottle he kept under the grease bin.

"I'm going to sell a book and get rich," I said.

"I'm going to get laid three hundred and sixty-five times," Gino said, winning our nickels with the ten of diamonds, a buxom tart bent over looking backward at the camera through her legs.

"What about you, kid?" Carlos asked me. He had little gold stars pasted all over his cheeks. "How many times do you plan to get laid next year?"

"I don't know, I don't have a girlfriend," I said, losing my third nickel to the artist's nine of clubs, a lewd nude wearing a top hat and high heels.

Gino acted incredulous. "How can you not have a girl in this city? There are more women here than stars across the sky. It's like an apple orchard with ten thousand trees and a thousand ripe apples on every tree begging to be picked. You're young like me, you're not bad looking, and you can speak English," he added. "There's no excuse not to have a novia."

"But I'm always broke," I explained self-consciously. "I can't even pay for dinner and a movie."

"'Broke'?" he exclaimed, even more disbelieving as he cupped his crotch with one hand and yanked upward. "Che, blondie, all you need is *this*."

Popeye chose that moment to stop at the stand with a woman named Martha on his arm. She had jumped right out of the deck of cards we were playing with. At least twice the sailor man's size, she had blue hair and a butterfly tattoo on one cheek. She was missing two front teeth and wore lipstick the color of Nehi orange soda pop.

"I love this guy," Martha shouted in English, pounding Popeye on the back. "He's the peppiest pup I ever met. Dumber than a bucket of hair, I'll admit. But still, I haven't had this much fun since the pigs ate my baby brother."

In Spanish, to Roldán, Popeye gasped, "Her tetas alone weigh more than you do, patrón."

"What'd he say?" Martha asked me. "You talk their lingo, don't you?"

I nodded. "A bit. But I don't understand when they speak slang."

"'Slang'?" Martha blustered. "Slang my ass. This little critter is an Einstein with his prick. Come on, sailor boy, let's go home, I'm hungry."

With a grunt, Martha picked Popeye up in a bear hug, backed out of the alley onto the sidewalk, put him down, lovingly cuffed the back of his head, and barked at us: "This bubba don't know the meaning of quit."

"Hey, Popeye," Carlos called hilariously in Spanish, "*don't fall in and drown.*"

Martha must have caught the drift because she bent over and fashioned a snowball the size of a grapefruit. She fired it through the half-open window at the artist but missed, nailing Roldán on the temple instead. He stumbled backward against the coffee percolator while large chunks of ice splashed and hissed as steam puffed up from the grease bin.

"*Auxilio!*" the boss cried. "Martians are attacking us!"

19. Men Without Women

Everything was quiet on January first. I felt antsy. From nine until noon I wrote a maudlin short story about a blind teenage guitarist visiting from Spain who got hit by a New York taxi and wound up in a hospital suffering from amnesia. The nurse who took care of him was practicing to be a flamenco dancer. She was beautiful but of course he couldn't see her. I didn't know how to end the story so it went into a pile on top of half a dozen other incomplete stories.

Time for a little break. Dressed extra-warm, I traipsed downstairs and said *"Buon giorno"* to Rocco, the super, who was hauling garbage cans out from the boiler room to the sidewalk. I offered to help but he grunted me off. *"Vada via."*

So I walked north on West Broadway to Washington Square. All around the dreary park, tree branches were spindly naked, very black, icy cold. The dirty snow was pockmarked by a million footprints. Somebody had built seven snowpeople inside the fountain, which gurgled water only in summertime.

A bus carried me up to Forty-seventh Street. My heart started beating faster six blocks before I got off. Nevertheless, I mustered the courage to walk west past the diamond exchange and a camera store to El Parrillón and found it closed. I was relieved and disappointed. Peering through the window, all I could see was a bar and many round tables covered by clean white linen. Where did Cathy and her parents live and what were they doing right now?

On my way back to Fifth Avenue I stopped at a pay phone, making a collect call to my folks to wish them a happy New

Year. We didn't talk long because it was too chilly not to be in motion.

I took a bus south from Forty-seventh Street to Madison Square where I got off and hiked the rest of the way downtown feeling excited, desperate, and hungry for more in life. I wanted Fame, Fortune, Sex, Love, and plenty of delicious food and high-class alcohol. I wanted to be married and fly around the world, visiting Paris, Rome, and Istanbul, maybe even Manila. Too bad the holiday season had ended.

Lo and behold, I bumped into Alfonso, Eduardo, and Luigi scurrying miserably north along MacDougal Street and we walked together up to the park. "Happy New Year," I said. "How are tricks with Adriana, La Petisa, Renata, and Sofía?" That was supposed to be a joke.

Eduardo didn't think so. He thought Adriana should have a scarlet A branded on the center of her forehead prior to being deported from this country for hooking without a license. The night before he had tried to pick up a girl at the Ninth Circle and she told him to "bug off." What did *that* mean? "I can hear Adriana cackling, the witch."

Alfonso explained, "It isn't her fault. It's just a puerile fixation inside your own adolescent head."

"Look who's talking," Eduardo grumbled. "The mugwump who can't decide whether to marry the sexpot devil or a humdrum saint."

"At least he has a choice." Luigi flicked his cigarette butt into the gutter. "La Petisa hates my face. She cooks, she keeps the apartment clean, but she won't even dole out kisses. I am treated like a eunuch in my own house. If I had a Sofía I'd be ecstatic."

"Stop." Alfonso held up one hand. "I feel so desperate I don't even want to talk about my novias."

But while we were circling the fountain like hamsters in an exercise wheel he said: "In her last letter Renata implied that she might start dating other men if I don't agree to marry her. My heart freezes when I think of that. It isn't fair. Why don't women play by the rules?"

And Eduardo still never mentioned the ten bucks he owed me.

20. I Am Beautiful

Though I wore a knitted cap, gloves, and my kapok jacket to the dance studio I half froze to death anyway. Jorge had on his porkpie hat and scarf and overcoat. Between numbers he shoved his hands into his crotch. Cathy started out wearing a sweater and a cap but shed them quickly. Even though our breath was visible in the chill air she became soaked from the dancing. I couldn't take my eyes off her. Certain moves within a bulerías or a solear were special. I sat far away and kept my mouth shut.

After the practice session Cathy said, "Let's go for coffee." We three walked through dirty snow to the Downtown Café and slipped into a booth. Jorge had a six-word vocabulary, even in his native Spanish. He came from Sevilla, Spain, and was now studying flamenco guitar with an exiled maestro named Alejandro Cárdenas.

The waitress brought over some coffees.

"Here you go," she said, taking them off her tray. "Three cups of ordinary joe brewed in our cool kitchen especially for you good people by little elves from Brazil."

Cathy said, "When I am a star I want to buy a house in Andalucía and another one in Buenos Aires. I'll keep a New York apartment but I don't like the United States."

She chain-smoked cigarettes. I said, "Isn't that bad for you?"

"No me importa. I'm young. They don't kill you for a while."

She ordered two glazed doughnuts with her coffee. I said, "Don't you have to watch your diet?"

"Not me, vos. I still have my girlish figure. But flamenco doesn't worry what size or shape you are as long as you have duende. Some of the greatest stars are elephants."

Her smile was dazzling, her bravado seductive. One minute she exuded a little-girl innocence, the next minute she could withdraw, suddenly haughty and professional.

"To be an artist you can't care about anyone except yourself," Cathy told me. "I can get away with murder because right now I am so beautiful."

Then she leaned forward and whispered: "Maybe I don't have a drop of gypsy blood, but my soul was born in Granada."

She drank one coffee and ordered a refill. Her skin was pale and her hair as shiny as wet coal. She wore bright red lipstick and thick mascara and her eyes had that mischievous sparkle. After practice she had donned an old sweatshirt and replaced the flamenco shoes with a dirty pair of fur-lined boots from Argentina. She had reapplied her makeup before leaving the dance studio. Now she clicked open a compact and checked her face again and then put on fresh lipstick. She fixed it by pressing her lips on a napkin and gave the napkin to me.

I asked her to sign the lipstick print and she wrote: *Con cariño, Catalina María Escudero.*

"Do you dream about me?" she teased. "I bet all you boys dream about me. I am a femme fatale. Before I am twenty-three I will make a Hollywood movie. Do you think I'm gorgeous?"

How could any man say no?

Cathy laughed and put a fresh cigarette between her lips. She snapped her fingers. "Give me fire, baby." She said *baby* in English.

With pleasure I struck a match.

When he wasn't playing guitar, Jorge seemed half asleep. He never said anything. Cathy talked to me about herself, her native Argentina, her spangled dancing. I listened, bewitched. Cathy prattled on. And Jorge tuned us out like an indifferent dumb animal basking in tropical sunshine.

21. Party Poopers

During the second week of January an Argentine boxer was slated to fight in Madison Square Garden. Roldán pasted a cartel of the bout on the brick wall beside the empanada stand. The Latin heavyweight was undefeated down south, having won six knockouts in a row since turning professional. He was going to battle an unknown American and no one doubted that he would clobber the bum. All the muchachos declared it would be "no contest."

Roldán seized on the event as an excuse for a party. He contacted a friend who had a pal who knew some people at the Garden who could sell us tickets for a reduced price. "And we'll have a dinner at my place before the knockout," he said. "I'll make sangría. And chicken in a spicy stew with pigs' knuckles and niños envueltos and papas rellenas."

"Dale," Carlos the Artist cried. "We'll get pissed to the gills and they'll have to carry us to the Garden! Better yet, we'll go in Popeye's diaper truck."

Everybody wanted a ticket.

Gino paid first and I followed suit because I had extra cash from unloading a furniture truck on Broome Street. Alfonso was next in line and promptly bet five dollars with Gino against his own countryman, whom he claimed had a glass chin. Luigi forked over the price of a ticket, as did Carlos the Artist. La Petisa refused to participate, calling us "barbarians." When we pressed Popeye to join us he said that nylons were not as profitable as advertised: He was broke. But Chuy sprang for four tickets, one for himself, one for Popeye, and two extras for as yet unselected women. Looking gaunt and deranged, Luigi's long-haired weight-lifting pal, El Coco, gave Roldán a dirty sock filled with pennies for his entrance fee.

Six nights before the bout Eduardo visited the empanada stand apoplectic because through binoculars he'd seen his ex-wife making out with her fat boyfriend near the window of her apartment without the shades drawn . . . and he also plunked down the price of admission.

On the day of the fight I only worked lunch at the Night Owl. Then I went to Roldán's messy digs and helped the fat man prepare our meal. His Christmas tree was still up, the little lights blinking. It was cold outside, the temperature not far above zero. By four o'clock we had two large kettles on the stove simmering and awaiting the onslaught. We made a sangría of red wine, sugar, and slices of melon, with oranges and also lemons. By five o'clock, when guests should have arrived, everything was ready. I lay down on the rumpled bed in Roldán's room and watched television for a spell and soon fell asleep to snowflakes ticking against the window. At six the cook's pudgy hand shook me awake.

"Where is everyone?" I asked.

"Only Chuy has come. But he brought two minas."

I sat up. Chuy was seated at the kitchen table facing a pair of teenagers, Angela and Adelita. He was preening and leaning close to their faces, murmuring sweet nothings.

"We might as well eat now," Roldán said. "Everything is ready and we won't reach the Garden on time if we delay any longer."

He lifted a lid and stirred with his serving spoon. We ate hearty and drank sangría, getting bloated and tipsy. Chuy described in gory detail the operations on his stump that were preparing it for a prosthetic hand. Angela and Adelita giggled, smoking cigarettes while they ate. Their funny off-color jokes caught us by surprise and we had a good dinner. A number 9 train carried us up to Madison Square Garden in plenty of time to see the Bull of the Pampas lose his first American showdown by a fourth-round TKO.

"That will ruin his career," Roldán said, disgusted.

Over the following days everyone stopped by the empanada stand with a brazen excuse—a girl, a last-minute job, an urgent obligation. Eduardo had worked overtime editing a newsreel about Cuba and the Soviet Union. El Coco got lost on the subway. Popeye couldn't make it because the diaper truck had a flat tire. Luigi had a fight with La Petisa because she declined to screw him. And Alfonso had spent all night typing a twelve-page letter to Renata thanking her for the gauche jester cap (that he'd already lost), followed by a two-paragraph bread-and-butter note to Sofía for the gloves (which he treasured).

The muchachos turned over their unused tickets, begging the fat man to obtain refunds. Roldán promised that he would try. Meanwhile, he brought the leftover food down from his apartment to the kiosk, and during the next week he dished out the vittles and sangría free to whoever was hungry. "It would have tasted better on Friday but it's still palatable," he insisted.

Gino refused to pay off the bet with Alfonso because "If *you* had lost you wouldn't have paid me, either. Just like everyone else in the patota."

"Not true," Alfonso said. "I'm the only honorable guy, besides Roldán, in our gang."

Gino said, "But you're always broke, profe. You never even give me a tip when I'm working here on the maestro's night off."

Alfonso retorted, "Oh? And how come I've never seen you hand the boss a tip when *he's* running the stand?"

"Because he's the boss," Gino said. "He rakes in all the profit. I'm only a hired hand."

Luigi said, "Che, profe won the bet. You better pay up."

"*You* pay up, you're so rich," Gino said. "Get the money from your loudmouth concubine, La Petisa."

Luigi was too small to attack Gino, so instead he opened his wallet and gave Alfonso five bucks.

Gino was appalled. "Wait a minute, you little monster. Are you trying to make me look bad?"

Luigi said, "You make yourself look worse than my face by acting like a pudenda."

"Fuck you, quemado." Gino pushed Luigi's five dollars back at him and slapped one of his own bills onto the counter in front of Alfonso. "And fuck you, too, profe. Go to hell both of you."

"Thank you," Alfonso said politely. "Now, who wants an empanada compliments of me? Don't be bashful, boys, I'm loaded."

22. Greta Garbo

Okay, it was "finished." Now I had to act. Into a manila envelope went my college romance novel. Along with the manuscript I included a self-addressed postcard so that the publishers could notify me of their rejection by mail. Then I would travel north and pick up my book, saving the cost of postage. After all, a subway token was only fifteen cents.

I spent an hour going over my list of publishers. Then I made a decision. The Lexington Avenue line took me to midtown Manhattan where I approached the front desk of my first choice. I explained to the receptionist about the postcard inside. She took the slim package from me and weighed it in her hands. "What have we here?" she smirked. "*Moby Dick? David Copperfield? The Brothers Karamazov?*"

I departed feeling breathless and humiliated. Back downtown, I hurried west on Bleecker Street as nervous and hungry as a wolf. When I turned the corner at the Figaro, Chuy's accountant, Greta Garbo, was standing at the kiosk's window nursing a cup of coffee while smoking a Tiparillo. She had on a fashionable overcoat and tall suede boots. To celebrate the submission of my novel I had decided to order a pork empanada. Eating it would be ecstasy.

"I want a pork empanada the size of the Empire State Building," I told the cocinero.

"I'll pay for the pie," Greta Garbo said. "It would be my pleasure."

I balked. "Oh no, thank you, but no."

She said, "I'm serious. You look like a starving artist to me."

"But I have *money*," I protested. I took out my wallet and showed her. "Yesterday I unloaded garment bales on Canal Street."

Greta Garbo said, "That's not money, it's chicken feed. Cookie crumbs."

While we were arguing, Eddie Ortega appeared at the window still wearing his black leather jacket and the red Converse All-Stars. Also blue jeans with rolled-up cuffs. That was his uniform. Roldán plucked a half dozen bills from the register drawer and handed them over. Eddie scribbled in his notebook. He said, "Gimme a pastelito," so the boss gave him a pastelito and a napkin. Eddie gobbled the treat, wiped off his fingers, and handed back the napkin.

As he departed Greta Garbo asked, "What was *that* all about?"

"None of your business," Roldán said. He flicked his fingertips scornfully.

To me, the accountant said, "I hear you think you're a writer. What do you write about?"

"I'm working on lots of stuff," I said. "But I haven't completed anything worthwhile."

"What sort of *stuff*?" she asked, blowing smoke in a thin stream up toward the stars. "Have you published anything?"

"No, not yet. I write novels and short stories. They aren't any good, though."

"Oh my, Mr. Self-Confidence. What sort of novels?" she persisted.

I didn't like talking about my work but feared even worse being impolite. Feeling squeamish, I said, "One is a college romance, another is about a Bowery bum. A third concerns the lives of a robber baron family on the North Shore of Long Island."

"How fascinating," she said, already bored.

Roldán wrapped a napkin around the bottom half of my empanada and set it on a paper plate. I took a bite and reached for the Tabasco sauce. The cook plucked Greta Garbo's five-dollar bill off the window ledge instead of my own. He gave her the change and she pointedly left him a one-dollar tip. My five-dollar bill just sat there.

"Have you ever read any books by Ernest Hemingway?" the accountant asked.

"Of course. I've read all his novels and short stories, plus *Death in the Afternoon*. He's my hero."

She said, "I think Hemingway was just a little boy with an enormous dick looking for a big fish to fuck."

Then she picked up my five-dollar bill and tucked it into my jacket pocket and trotted off to call a cab.

23. Inside, Outside

A strange thing happened. I was standing in the kiosk's alley watching TV, hemmed against the wall by Carlos the Artist, when Cathy Escudero and Jorge appeared at the window. Roldán slid it open a third. Cathy had on a green Santa Claus cap with a white pom-pom and her shabby overcoat. Jorge wore the porkpie hat and carried his guitar case. He had no gloves and seemed half frozen to death.

"Come on in," the fat man said, turning down the TV sound. He added in English: "Baby, it's cold outside." For two weeks I had been teaching him to say that.

Carlos pushed open the door and, after stamping snow off her feet, Cathy came inside. Jorge stayed on the sidewalk.

"Dale, dale," Roldán said. "You look like a frozen Popsicle."

Jorge held up one hand to indicate that he felt more comfortable exactly where he was. He continued smoking a cigarette.

Cathy said, "We each want a pork empanada and a cup of hot coffee with a top. In a bag to go, please. How are you, blondie? And what are your friends' names, if I may be so bold?"

"I am Carlos the Artist," Carlos said. "And this is the boss himself, Don Áureo Roldán."

"Mucho gusto conocerles," Cathy said, shaking hands with them both and doing a double take on the artist's getup. He had on a top hat and a bullfighting cape, and a third eye was carefully painted in the middle of his forehead. "What kind of artist are you, Carlito, a bullshit artist?"

Carlos replied, "No, I'm a professional womanizer. But you're not my type. I prefer girls that have graduated from kindergarten."

Roldán said quickly, "He's only joking. He's really a good artist. He's having a show uptown in the spring."

"What kind of show?" Cathy asked. "Finger painting? Connecting the dots with crayons?"

Roldán said, "Oíme, nene, at least put the guitar inside." He was talking to Jorge, who had never set down the guitar case. "Your hand will fall off in this cold."

Jorge said, "On the street I never let go of my guitar."

So Roldán left the window open. Cathy coughed from the empanada smoke. "He's the best flamenco guitarist in New York City," she bragged. "Isn't that right, blondie?"

I leaned forward, my head turned sideways so I could see her past Carlos. "That's right," I said.

Carlos wanted Jorge to play a song. "Play 'Bésame Mucho,' kid."

"He only plays flamenco," Cathy said. "He doesn't sing. He's a purist, not a sentimental puppy dog."

Embarrassed, Jorge turned his back on the window, staring at a slant across MacDougal to Dante's Café. How did he keep from shivering?

Carlos said, "I heard flamenco was invented by retarded gypsies in order to make fun of themselves."

Fast as he could, Roldán folded napkins around the empanadas, wrapped them with tinfoil, then carefully placed them in a small brown paper bag. He added clean napkins and put tops on the coffee cups and dropped two creamers and sugar packets into the sack, along with a thin plastic swizzle stick to stir the coffees.

Cathy paid, put a quarter tip on the counter, told Jorge to take the sack off the window ledge, and pressed backward out the door holding the coffee cups.

She paused at the window. "Thank you, maestro. Toodle-oo, blondie. Adiós, Carlos the Artist, don't get your cape caught in a fan blade."

The boss closed his window. Three seconds later Carlos said, "Who was that uppity viper?"

I could tell, however, that he liked her.

"She's not a viper," I said.

24. Cops and Sobbers

Uh-oh. Eduardo's ex-wife, Adriana, descended from a taxi and walked purposefully into the empanada stand as if she owned it, trapping Luigi, El Coco, and me in the alley. She had on a Russian imitation-rabbit-fur hat and a spiffy leather overcoat with a turned-up collar. Her face looked very gaunt and pale and her lipstick was a shade of crimson so bright it almost hurt our eyes. The high tension crackling off her body gave all three of us goose bumps. She stuck a cigarette between her lips and ignored the match Luigi struck, clicking open her own lighter. Adriana exhaled into Roldán's face, saying, "Qué tal, pelotudos?" That's when we knew she was plastered.

"We're not assholes," Luigi said. "We're just lonely guys looking for a bit of warmth and laughter to mitigate the horrors of this cold, cruel world."

"You're assholes in my book," Adriana said. "Where is Eduardo, the chief asshole in this city of assholes, which is the asshole capital of the Western Hemisphere?"

The cook asked politely, "Querés tomar algo?"

Adriana ignored him and addressed me. "Let me ask you something, blondie. You don't have a Latin temperament. You're very slow like a caracol. You're probably still a virgin. That haircut reminds me of an aircraft carrier. I bet if you ever get married you'll be faithful to your wife. So tell me: How come you hang out with this pack of oversexed dogs who always treat women like shit?"

Because I didn't understand the word *caracol*, I asked, "What is a caracol?"

Before Adriana could explain, El Coco unleashed a startling tirade: "Go away, you Nazi. Leave us alone. We were having fun here until you came along and stunk up the kiosk like a fart. Maybe the devil thinks you're pretty but you look like lizard crap to me."

Adriana paused with the cigarette held pensively in front of her cheek. El Coco was wearing a threadbare hooded parka and gloves with the fingers cut off. His unruly black beard reminded me of Rasputin.

Finally, Adriana belched, checked her watch, and addressed Roldán: "Fijate, tubby, it's nine P.M.—time to close. So why don't you grab your human mop over there in the corner and clean up this dump?"

Luigi said, "I know it's impolite to speak harshly with a woman, so please forgive me in advance. But why don't you shut your stupid mouth?"

Adriana did not hesitate even a beat. "Why don't *you* put your face between two slices of a sesame bun and call it a hamburger, charcoal man?"

Roldán lunged against the counter trying to grab Luigi but he wasn't quick enough—the burnt man slapped Adriana.

She broke apart, bursting into tears, and banged backward out of the alley shrieking. Then she stood on the sidewalk exercising her lungs like a drowning lady on the *Titanic*.

Some disheveled beatniks came out of the Hip Bagel. Other pedestrians stopped, inspecting Adriana curiously. Her shrill Spanish invective drew two cops on horseback who galloped down MacDougal Street, dismounted at the kiosk, and gaped at her. One of them shouted, "What the hell happened here?"

Luigi explained in Spanish, "She's drunk. She's insulting everybody. So I hit her."

The cops asked me, "What did he say?"

Before I could think I translated his words, so they arrested Luigi, clicking on handcuffs, and called for a squad car on their walkie-talkies. Two dozen tourists had gathered to watch the fun. Roldán was standing there in his filthy apron and beside him El Coco looked like a derelict that had just crawled out of a rathole. Adriana kept hollering invective at Luigi and Eduardo at the top of her voice. Eventually she spit at one cop so they manacled her too, treating her roughly in the process. By now two cruisers had arrived with their cherry tops blinking. They blocked traffic on MacDougal below Bleecker. Luigi and Adriana were hustled to the rear seats of separate squad cars and Adriana shouted more obscenities about Eduardo. An officer finally asked me, "Who the hell is Eduardo?"

"Her ex-husband."

"And who's the burnt marshmallow?"

I summoned the courage to reply, "He is not a burnt marshmallow."

The cop rolled his eyes. "Excuse me, sir. Let me rephrase my question. Who is the handsome little man wearing the bomber jacket?"

"He's just a friend. He didn't do anything. She's crazy when she drinks."

The cop snorted. "I hate to tell you, but everybody in this city is crazy, even when they don't drink."

"Luigi's a good guy," I insisted timidly. "Where are you taking him?"

"None of your damn business."

The squad cars drove away, the crowd dispersed, and soon enough the police horses clip-clopped south toward their stables below Canal Street.

Luigi arrived at the kiosk on the following night none the worse for wear. "Adriana is like an atomic bomb," he said, laughing. "I like that in a woman."

25. An Impromptu Diatribe

"That empanada stand is a silly place," Cathy said to me. "It's a club for little boys to hang out in who don't want to grow up. The men in my country are all like that. The fat man who owns the joint is a child. And that friend of yours, 'Carlos the Artist,' is a goofy numskull. Who does he think he is, Cantinflas? If you spend too much time there with those infants you'll turn into an adolescent basket case yourself, a real boludo. You'll even begin to look like an empanada. And one day you'll just be standing on the sidewalk minding your own business when somebody will walk up behind you and shake half a bottle of Tabasco sauce onto your head."

I don't know what had prompted the diatribe. She and Jorge had been working on a solear, which was stern and slow moving at the start. You had to enter it carefully, with constraint and melancholia and deliberate moves that were dream-like and ponderous. The effect was created not by flashy footwork or by explosions of artistic zeal, but rather by a slow liberation of dire emotion translated through minimal guitar work and careful dance moves.

Abruptly, Cathy had stopped, put her hands on her hips, and delivered to me the curt dissertation on the kiosk.

"But I *like* the empanada stand," I said.

Cathy frowned at me. Then she told Jorge to begin again at the top, which he did, and they continued the practice session.

26. C Rations

Alfonso said, "His stupid publisher was driving the car too fast. The world mourns when a great artist like that is taken away too soon."

He was talking about Albert Camus. The accident had occurred in 1960, when Camus was forty-six.

Luigi said, "Carlos Gardel was only forty-eight when that plane crash burned him alive."

Roldán said, "I don't think Van Gogh was even forty when he shot himself." He stuck wooden spoons into little cups of dulce de leche, handing a complimentary cup to each of us.

"You're right, cocinero." Alfonso reached over to shake the fat man's hand. "He was thirty-seven. He died in 1890, one year before Rimbaud."

Luigi banged his own forehead. "How can you remember those dates, profe?"

Alfonso made a cavalier gesture. "I also remember when García Lorca was shot by the Guardia Civil. August 19, 1936. He was only thirty-eight years old. Spain murdered its own heart when those bastards did that."

Popeye double-parked the diaper truck on MacDougal Street. Carlos the Artist jumped from the passenger side and opened the rear doors. He and Popeye brought over two cardboard cartons that they set on the window ledge and Popeye slit them open with a linoleum cutter. A bold black logo on the boxes said U.S. ARMY SURPLUS. Carlos was decked out in a black beret, black cape, black silk blouse, black trousers, and black boots with elevated heels. He also wore sunglasses and green lipstick, and was smoking a Gitane.

Luigi said, "Mirá, here's two clowns from Transylvania."

The sailor man ignored him, prying forth several drab C-ration kits which he set dramatically on the window ledge. One kit offered ham with pineapple and angel food cake. Another had Spam and beans and cherry Jell-O. A third contained meatloaf and chocolate pudding.

Roldán said, "Where did you find those fossils, boys?"

Popeye raised his hands in protest. "Please, don't ask. It's a delicate question and nobody's business. Watch this."

He removed a can, fit a tin key in the lid tab, twisted the metal band off, removed the top, and extended the ham with pineapple toward Roldán: "Go ahead, cookie, pruebalo."

Roldán eyeballed the meal with obvious distaste and suspicion.

"How old is that, marinero—World War II?"

"Nope, Korea. Do me a favor, *taste* it. This crap is good."

"Good for parrots and rats," Alfonso said. "*You* taste it."

"Hey, why not?" Popeye probed with a plastic government-issue fork, gouging free a chunk, and ate it, chewing thoughtfully. Then he brightened. "Man, this is *wonderful*, no kidding."

Meanwhile, Carlos had opened the angel food cake. "This is almost a culinary treasure from Paris." But when he turned the tin upside down a shriveled thumb-sized nugget of stale pastry clanged off the window ledge, bounced onto the sidewalk, and rolled across into the gutter.

"You can sell these dinners as snacks to tourists," Popeye urged the cocinero. "Fifty cents apiece. You keep two bits and I get a quarter to split with my partner here. It's all on consignment, no risk. I'll trust you to be honest."

Alfonso said, "You couldn't give away that stuff to a starving Armenian."

"Screw you." Popeye pleaded: "Oíme, patrón. I'm so broke my balls are falling off. And my partner here hasn't sold a painting in eight months. One day he'll be more famous than Picasso. But right now we're both in deep shit."

"How many cartons do you have in that truck?" the boss asked.

"One hundred."

"Don't do it," Luigi warned. "They'll arrest you for poisoning the public."

Roldán studied Popeye and Carlos for a few seconds. Then he said, "I'll take eight boxes for starters."

Popeye jumped for joy and ran over to fetch them. Carlos admitted, "To be honest, maestro, even a pig couldn't eat this swill."

The cook replied, "I know. But you misfits are friends of mine."

I said, "James Dean was only twenty-four when he died in a car crash."

They looked at me, puzzled.

27. Rude People

I asked Alfonso to come see Cathy Escudero and Jorge with me. "They're so talented you will be amazed." Sporadic snowflakes dogged us on the way over. A few old Christmas trees with shreds of tinsel were lying beside garbage cans. I felt glum because two more short-story rejection slips had arrived in the mail.

Adding insult to injury, Alfonso complained, "Flamenco is crude and brutal. It's abrupt and nerve-shattering. Like bullfighting, full of blood and pretentious acrobatics. It doesn't belong in Argentina. I prefer what is melancholy and beautiful—for example the tango, which doesn't bash you to smithereens with obnoxious flamboyance."

We ascended in the Fourteenth Street elevator and walked down the hallway. I placed my hand on the doorknob: "Are you finished, profe, or is there anything else you want to get off your chest?" Through the door we could hear Jorge's guitar and Cathy's noisy stomping.

Alfonso said, "I'll spare you, blondie. I'm feeling compassionate."

I opened the door and we tip-toed inside, taking a seat at my customary spot against the east wall of the studio. Cathy had chopsticks through her bun and a yellow fringed scarf around her shoulders. She was practicing with the scarf, suddenly grabbing it and twisting underneath, flashing the thing quickly like a bullfighting cape and then landing it magically against her shoulders and neck again. To me the routine seemed graceful and I was sure Alfonso would be impressed.

But he grew fidgety. Of course the studio was cold. Yet our warmth, or at least Cathy's heat, had put condensation on the windows. Nevertheless, you could see every breath on the frigid air.

Alfonso was not enthralled by the dancing or by the music, and his lips turned blue. After ten minutes as a spectator he leaned close to whisper: "My balls are totally shrunk. Yo ya me voy."

My pal stood up and marched out.

Cathy quit dancing. "Who the hell was that?"

"A friend," I explained nervously. "He got cold. That sarape he wears is stupid for a New York winter. It couldn't keep him warm in the Amazon. But he's a mathematician and too poor to buy a proper jacket."

"Where's he from?" she asked. "The Soviet Union? He looks like a communist. I don't like him."

"Actually, he lives in Buenos Aires. He's on scholarship here studying at NYU."

"He was rude to me."

"Not deliberately. His manner seems abrupt because he's timid. But his heart is as big as China."

Cathy said, "Who are you, his fucking agent?"

"Excuse me?"

The dancer barked an order at Jorge, who started playing again. Cathy walked around impatiently waiting for the proper moment to hop back into the dance like a schoolgirl planning to reenter a sidewalk game of jump rope.

When next I met Alfonso at the empanada stand I asked, "What happened at the dance studio? Why were you so impolite?"

"I know that girl, blondie. She waited on me at El Parrillón on Forty-seventh Street."

"What were you doing up there?"

"I wanted to eat a lot of barbecued meat and be constipated for three days."

"How could you afford it? You never have any money."

"That's right, but you forget I'm a gaucho at heart. So at times price is no object."

"Well, what happened?"

"Nothing. I ate a lot of barbecued meat and was constipated for three days."

"I mean with Cathy Escudero."

"She was rude. She acted like a prima donna, not a waitress. With her nose stuck up in the air. She's got an Anna Magnani complex. And she never cracked a smile."

"Maybe she hates her job," I said.

"Everybody hates their job, kid. That's no reason to be a sourpuss."

"Don't you think she's beautiful?" I asked.

"Of course, but so what?"

Alfonso stuck an index finger into his hot chocolate mug, scooping out a sugary brown film near the bottom. He licked it off carefully. All the destitute boys who visited the empanada stand were like that. Food was precious and they devoured every last bit of it.

"She's also a good dancer," I said.

"In Buenos Aires? Maybe."

"What does that mean?"

"In Spain they'd throw tomatoes."

That put a damper on our conversation.

Alfonso draped a conciliatory arm around my shoulders. "No te preocupés," he said. "Women are like cats. Either you cotton to them or you don't. My Renata is worse than that ersatz flamenco dancer. She loves to argue for argument's sake, and nothing is worse than a female sophist enamored of specious altercation. It's exhausting. She throws away money like a millionaire even if she only has twenty pesos. My other girlfriend, Sofía, is frugal and never confrontational. She's pregnant with common sense and compassionate spirituality, a regular Teresa of Ávila. She also wants children, as I do. Renata thinks kids are a filthy mucus that should be flushed down the toilet. She's more like Hedda Gabler."

He paused, reflecting on his two women.

"But it's Renata I'm crazy about even though she drives me crazy."

28. Tiny Brains

I entered the Mexican Village restaurant on Thompson Street chased by a gust of frigid wind. I had extra cash from running errands for the messenger service on Sixth Avenue near Charlton. I sat down next to La Petisa and Popeye who were halfway through a meal of enchiladas, refried beans, and red wine. They were in high spirits. The waiter brought me a wineglass.

Popeye filled it as he said, "We are celebrating our noviada. I've inherited the five languages from Luigi."

"I told Luigi good-bye," La Petisa said. "One more day of the festering place he calls his pad and I would have gone bonkers. El Coco walked in on me when I was taking a shower and didn't even apologize. Of course, I have exchanged Luigi for a man who rolls his underwear into tiny bundles. I press them with an iron to make them pretty, but he immediately scrunches them up into balls. He claims he learned this from the navy and it keeps his clothing neat. Neat? Caramba! I also make him wear a shirt in bed because those tattoos are disgusting. And when is he going to buy some *teeth*?"

I said, "Hey, don't be so mean. It isn't po—"

"Don't worry, kid," Popeye interrupted. "She's not even firing BBs. These teeth were knocked out by a Singapore hooker. An Italian puta once stole my wallet, my bell-bottoms, *and* my seaman's card. An Egyptian slut stabbed me in the buttocks with a hat pin. I am used to the abuse of women. In fact, I like it as long as they give me the Little Clamshell in return."

I summoned the courage to address La Petisa: "Well, you go with a lot of guys. Don't you ever want to stay with one person?"

"I do the same thing with countries," she said. "That's how I like it. Every nation I visit has the most fabulous geography . . . hasta me encuentro podrida de aburrimiento. Then I move on. But always I learn a lot. I've had an incredible education."

I asked, "But are you happy?"

"Am I *happy*? Sometimes yes, sometimes no, but that isn't the important part."

"You're always in motion," I said. "Maybe you never stay long enough to understand the place you are in or the person you are with."

La Petisa laughed. "Aren't *you* loquacious today, my friend." Then she bent close to me. "I understand *motion*, blondie. My soul wants to keep *moving*. Like a bee collecting pollen. I'm storing up memories now so that later when I am an old bag with arthritis I can nibble on the honeycombs composed of all my adventures. Capeesh?"

I said, "Of course," just as a cardboard box hurled by the wind hit a nearby window. We all jumped.

Popeye said, "It's simple, nene. God gave us genitals for a reason. I got laid for the first time when I was eleven years old. My grandpa paid for it. The last thing I'll do on my deathbed is make some bumptious amazon happy. Meanwhile, I have La Petisa and she has me, a collaboration made in heaven."

La Petisa winked at me, reaching under the table as she leaned forward to kiss Popeye: "This man is such a child, blondie. His brains are the size of a fingernail."

Popeye grinned. "So what? The last time I checked, my prick didn't have a cerebellum."

29. Intellectuals

When next I visited the dance studio, Cathy asked, "Where's your communist novio from the Soviet Union?" She grabbed a small towel from her tote bag and wiped her forehead. I had just taken my spot against the wall to watch them practice. Jorge was replacing a broken guitar string.

"I don't know," I said. "Maybe in class at NYU. Or grading student papers."

"He's a jackass," she said. "Mr. Superior. A xenophobe. I bet he hates anything Spanish."

I smiled and tipped my head a little, noncommittal.

Cathy told Jorge, "Hurry up, maestro, I'm getting cold. I'm all wet. I don't want to freeze to death."

Jorge took nail clippers from his guitar case and cut off the end of the new nylon string. He tightened the wooden tuning peg while Cathy walked around impatiently, swinging her arms back and forth to keep them limber. She had put on her overcoat as soon as they stopped.

"I don't like intellectuals, blondie. They read too many books. They're afraid of life. They live vicariously."

"I know what you mean," I said.

Cathy put her hands on her hips and regarded me. Something changed. Her eyes brightened and her cheeks suddenly glowed; her demeanor was altered completely. She filled up with light, her skin gleaming, fevered in a way that was almost celestial. I was startled and began to get aroused. After a moment she said, "You're a very patient person. I like your blue eyes."

"Thank you," I said.

"But you're too polite with women, blondie. You act like a scaredy-cat. I want to kick you to wake you up."

I said, "I'm awake."

Jorge said, "Listo," and played an arpeggio to prove it.

"Okay, back to work." Cathy took off her overcoat and dropped it on top of the tote bag. She told Jorge, "Start playing. I'll come in on the llamada."

He began to play while Cathy listened, tapping her toe in compás until suddenly he paused and then hit the llamada with six fast downward strokes and Cathy erupted, shouting, "Watch this, blondie!" as she swirled into the dance with a great lust to be perfect.

30. No Illusions

I got fired at the Night Owl Café because they were closing for renovations. I also received another short-story rejection slip and a rejection postcard from publisher number two. When I showed up at the empanada stand only Luigi, El Coco, and Roldán were there listening to a melancholy Carlos Gardel record on the Victrola. Greenwich Village was deserted and Roldán had sold only six empanadas, a pastelito, and two Cokes all evening.

Luigi was hunched way down with his bomber jacket collar turned up. He was smoking a cigarette like Jean-Paul Belmondo.

El Coco had on his filthy hooded parka and his gloves with the fingers chopped off. His unruly black beard probably harbored bedbugs and silverfish. He could have been a refugee from the trenches at Verdun during World War I.

"I'm tired," Luigi said. "I hate my job at the library. Why do I bet on the horses? I got drunk again last night and had another fight with a stranger. I always win because they're afraid to beat me up. And whenever I look in the mirror I see Bela Lugosi playing a vampire or Frankenstein."

Gardel sang:

> When you're not with me,
> I can't smell the flowers,
> I can't hear birds singing,
> And the night is so cold.

Roldán lifted the coffeepot. "Want me to hit you again?"

"Yeah." Luigi nudged his cup forward two inches and the fat man refilled it. "Gracias."

I asked, "How come you're in such a good mood?"

"Because La Petisa dumped me. You know *why* she dumped me? Because she couldn't stand my friend El Coco. You know why else? Because I am gorgeous like Clark Gable and she wanted a more ordinary-looking man, like that toothless loser Popeye. Of course, I wouldn't be so jealous if she had screwed me at least a few times."

He wrinkled his lip and ventured a sip of coffee.

Then he said, "Dale, blondie, let's take a stroll. I need more smokes."

We said good-bye to the fat man and headed north on MacDougal. El Coco followed along behind us like a hunchback from Notre Dame. Snow had melted away completely yet the city felt clammy and cold. All the buildings seemed old and shabby and garbage littered the sidewalks. Luigi had only one cigarette left, but Johnny had closed the Italian Newsstand early.

Luigi grumbled, "See how my luck is going? We'll probably have to walk a mile for a Camel."

While we marched along the burnt man talked about his life.

"I'm not a large man, kid, but I used to be in shape. Before the accident I had an okay mug. I come from a middle-income family, we had money. I loved the university. I had minas galore but they were not important to me. What's the expression in English? Profe told me: 'Find 'em, feel 'em, fuck 'em, forget 'em.' Las muchachas were a great diversion, nothing more."

We crossed Sixth Avenue to the Shamrock Bar which had a cigarette machine. Luigi thumbed in a quarter, pulled a lever, and scooped up the pack. He lit two cigarettes and gave one to El Coco. We departed the bar and headed south toward the empanada stand. Some teenagers were playing basketball under the lights at the Fourth Street playground.

Luigi said, "Then one night I lost my face in an explosion and, obviously, life changed."

"What kind of explosion?"

"I was putting gas in my father's car while also smoking a cigarette. Something happened, but I don't remember. I woke up at the hospital. Months later they sent me to this country."

"But you never had any operations?"

"I'm not stupid, blondie. They couldn't do beans with my face, even in America. They take skin off your ass and put it on your 'cheeks.' They transplant hair for your eyebrows. They shoot your lips full of plastic foam. You just exchange one type of gargoyle for another. But I like better this one, I'm used to it. The mask is inoperable and I'd go crazy if I nurtured illusions."

He stopped, tilted his head back, and squeezed out the eyedrops.

I said, "You're not a gargoyle."

El Coco said, "Man, that was a good cigarette. Can I have another?"

Luigi tapped one from the pack and lit it for him. El Coco said, "Gracias," turned around, and walked west.

At the kiosk Roldán was trying to close up but Eduardo's ex-wife, Adriana, was bending his ear, sober tonight yet pissed off. Yesterday she'd learned that Eduardo had been seen eating a pastrami sandwich beside one of his co-workers, a female with a bouffant hairdo, in Bryant Park behind the library.

"What do you care?" Luigi reasoned. "You're seeing another guy."

"I was married to Eduardo for six years. He's like a cyst in my heart. No matter who I date, the ache is always Eduardo. However, an elemental dinosaur like you would never understand."

Then she handed Luigi the bail money he'd put up for her two weeks ago and stalked away from us.

31. The Man from Uruguay

Suddenly another guy showed up at the dance studio on Fourteenth Street. He was older and wore sharp clothes, shiny boots, a tailored overcoat. Long curly hair bounced against his shoulders. His name was Aurelio Porta, and I soon learned he came from Montevideo, Uruguay. He was connected to the Manhattan consulate. Taking a seat on the floor beside me, he smoked black tobacco cigarettes while Cathy Escudero practiced.

At each session Jorge was better on the guitar. The minute he struck his first chord he came alive. His concentration stayed total. The second he quit playing he regressed into a chain-smoking zombie at a complete loss for words. During the practice he and Cathy talked only about problems of choreography in a curt, professional Spanish. They paid no attention to me and Aurelio Porta.

Aurelio nodded his head and did palmas to the beat, softly, always in compás. He sang under his breath in a hoarse gypsy manner. Cathy and Jorge practiced until both of them were so exhausted they could barely walk outside. Cathy complained that her feet hurt and her back was killing her and she had a headache.

Aurelio told her that she ought to slow it down a trifle during the display part of alegrías. Also, she had missed a llamada important to solear. Her arms should have extended higher and been bent more at the wrist during a certain passage of the tango. And it was too cute and showy when she clapped her hands and slapped her thighs at a particular moment of siguiriyas.

Cathy listened to him politely and never mouthed off or protested or defended herself. Carelessly, Aurelio reached for the back of her neck and massaged it a little.

We stopped at the Downtown Café where Cathy talked about her life and the rest of us listened. Our waitress brought over three coffees and a mocha java for Aurelio Porta, with whipped cream on top and cinnamon powder. "We had this one flown in special from Disneyland," the waitress said.

Cathy said, "As soon as I have money I'll buy my dad a Cadillac convertible. I want a swimsuit from Saks and a wedding ring from Tiffany's. I plan to be married six times. Do you guys like this eye shadow? It's from Italy." She turned her head. "Do you think my profile is elegant?"

"I think you are very elegant," Aurelio said. "But you shouldn't put quite as much rouge on your cheeks—it's tacky. As for the eye shadow from Italy, it looks like mud. Brown isn't your color. You'd be better off with something green or gray, not as dark, and more misty."

Cathy laughed and flicked her finger coyly against his chin. "Will you buy me some new eye shadow, Mr. Know-it-all?"

"Of course."

"He's rich," Cathy said to me, nodding at the distinguished Señor Porta. "He could walk into Tiffany's and buy out the entire ground floor. With enough change left over to purchase a palace in Madrid."

When the rich man smiled he seemed like a clever snake about to swallow a sparrow's egg.

Cathy bummed a cigarette from Aurelio and said, "I'm having trouble with solear. It's too moody for me. I hate that transition to bulerías halfway through. It feels wrong. I'm good at the speedy complex stuff, but when it's too slow I get nervous. I want to be energetic like a pistol shot."

Aurelio said, "Work on what you hate, and then for that dance alone you will become famous."

Cathy pouted and reiterated her previous complaint. "Flamenco is killing me. My feet ache, my ankles hurt, I have shin splints. My back is a disaster case. I wish I was dead."

"The greatest dancers end every night in the arms of death," Aurelio said. "And they wake up every morning afire like the sun."

Cathy grinned. "I'm like a hot little sunflower," she boasted. "Don't fly too close to me or I'll burn your wings and you'll fall into the ocean."

When we were ready to leave the café Aurelio Porta was first on his feet and he pulled back Cathy's chair. "Gracias," she said, plunging her hands deep into the pockets of her shabby overcoat and walking ahead of us.

"That girl has a strut," Aurelio commented approvingly.

Neither Jorge nor I answered him.

A blast of wind swept away Aurelio's hat. It bounced into the damp street and was immediately squashed by a car tire. I started after the hat, but Aurelio called me back.

"Let it go," he said, laughing. "I can easily buy another one."

32. Death of El Coco

Then El Coco died. That was a shock. Luigi came home and found his body in the bathtub half underwater. The medical examiner concluded it was a heart attack. El Coco had no bank account, no possessions except for the barbells, and only eleven dollars when his pockets were emptied.

"No tengo ni un mango," Luigi told us at the empanada stand. "What am I going to do?"

"Let the city consign him to a pauper's grave at Potter's Field," Alfonso said.

Even with such a charred face, Luigi blanched. "Are you crazy? He was a pal of mine."

"Also an Argentine," Roldán reminded us. "We should take care of our own."

Alfonso said, "He never talked to us. He hated women. What was his real name?"

"Dagoberto Hoffman," Luigi said.

"Does he have family down south?"

"No. When he left the patria he wiped the slate clean. He was never going back."

"How did you come to be friends?"

Embarrassed, Luigi stiffened a little. "I met him at a bar. The Page One."

"That place is Sodom and Gomorrah," Alfonso noted.

"Nevertheless, that's where we met. He was homeless at the time."

The fat man asked, "Was El Coco religious? If not, we should take up a collection to have him cremated."

Alfonso dug deep and placed a bill on the counter. "Here's ten bucks. That's all I have right now."

I also contributed a ten even though it hurt.

Roldán removed a twenty from the cash register, adding to the pile. Luigi stared at the money. The burnt face made it impossible for him to shed tears, but we could tell he was moved.

Alfonso said, "Dale, go ahead, take it."

That night Roldán put a jar on the counter for donations to El Coco's cremation fund. The rest of us began to spread the word.

La Petisa was upset about the cremation. "He wore a cross around his neck. He should have a proper burial. You're sending him straight to hell."

"*Tais toi*," Alfonso said, "and give us some money. Pretend you have a conscience."

She forked over twenty bucks, still protesting. "He should be buried at a Christian site with his barbells. He was a sweet and considerate man who never spoke ill of anyone. He was a gentle creature, timid and shy, not at all blasphemous like the rest of you infidels. He never tried to hump me and he was always polite."

"I don't want your fucking money," Luigi said. "Take it back. Go buy some panties and lipstick for Popeye."

Alfonso clapped his palm atop La Petisa's hand as she reached for her cash. "Don't be a nincompoop, Luigi."

La Petisa removed her hand. Luigi picked up the twenty and ripped it to shreds.

Gino said, "I never liked that guy. I think he was a puto."

According to Alfonso, "That's immaterial now. Hand over some loot."

Gino balked. "El Coco hated women, you know."

"I do, too," Alfonso said. "Now, open your wallet."

Gino said, "Screw you," and parted with five bucks.

Alfonso said, "That's not enough. Blondie gave ten and he's not even from Argentina."

"Try and take a penny more from me, profe."

"I don't want his fucking money," Luigi said.

"This isn't about you," Alfonso said, "it's about El Coco. Grow up."

Luigi tore Gino's five-spot into little pieces.

Popeye said, "I'd contribute ten dollars but that jealous asshole would just tear it up."

"No he won't," Alfonso promised. "I've had a talk with him."

Popeye was adamant. "I don't trust him. He's crazy."

"No I'm not," Luigi said. "I learned my lesson. Now, give me the ten bucks."

"Fuck you."

Carlos the Artist gave fourteen dollars. He remembered, "I had a conversation with El Coco once."

"What about?"

"He asked me to buy a dress for him at S. Klein's."

"What did you do?" Gino was horrified.

"I bought the dress. What's wrong with that?"

Eduardo wrote a check for four hundred dollars. Luigi almost fell over backward. "I don't need four hundred dollars. Are you crazy?"

"I don't *have* four hundred dollars," Eduardo said. "The check will bounce because there's only twenty-nine bucks in my account. Good. Then I'll be arrested and deported and I'll be rid of Adriana. This city is too small for both of us."

"Quit drinking," Alfonso suggested. "Pull yourself together, nene. Stop smoking marijuana."

Chuy surprised us all. "How much more do you need to light the fire?"

"Eighty-seven dollars."

The rich gigolo pulled a roll from his pocket, and, pressing it against his hip with the stump of his left wrist, he peeled off five twenties.

"I liked that guy," Chuy said.

Gino asked, "Why?"

"Because he had a lot more guts than you do."

After Luigi took care of the cremation details he returned to the kiosk asking, "What shall we do with the ashes?"

Alfonso said, "El Coco loved America. Let's take him to the Statue of Liberty."

"Are we allowed to do that?"

"Only in America."

Everybody agreed to carry the ashes on a ferryboat over to the Statue of Liberty where we would scatter them.

"I will bring an Argentine flag," Carlos the Artist vowed. "And some Rimbaud for the eulogy."

"I'll steal some holy water," La Petisa said.

"I don't want your holy water," Luigi said.

Gino's job was to locate a Bible.

"Fuck your Bible," Luigi said.

Chuy would supply the flowers.

And Eduardo planned to attend the obsequies so he could gather ideas for his own funeral.

But at the appointed hour only Alfonso, Roldán, Luigi,

and I showed up at the Battery and boarded the Staten Island Ferry with El Coco's ashes. Luigi was relieved. "If La Petisa or Gino or the marinero had showed up, I wouldn't have got on the boat."

A bright sun was shining on this first day of spring which still felt like winter. A pretty mist was lifting off the cold water. Seagulls made a racket around us. Roldán was bundled up like an enormous walrus wearing galoshes and wool-lined leather mittens in addition to his raccoon coat. Luigi had on two ratty sweaters, gloves, and a funny ski cap. But Alfonso had donned only his silly thin serape and the purple scarf. Not only had he lost Renata's obnoxious hat, but he had misplaced Sofía's gloves as well. His teeth chattered all the way over and back.

Afterward, stepping off the ferryboat onto Manhattan, Roldán slipped and crashed to the pavement. Grimacing, he clutched his wrist. *"Ouch!"*

We grappled him onto his feet and a taxi rushed us up to St. Vincent's Hospital where X-rays revealed that the wrist had been fractured. Two hours later we hit the sidewalk as darkness fell and it began to snow once more in the winter without end. Roldán was wearing a cast.

We aimed east along Greenwich, crossed Sixth Avenue onto Eighth Street, and stopped at the Orange Julius stand. Invited by the fat man, each of us ordered a Julius with an egg and a hot dog that we gobbled hungrily as we moseyed south past the Jungle Tap Room and crossed to Washington Square. Streetlamps in the empty park cast circles of harsh light interrupted by falling snowflakes.

We halted. Roldán, Alfonso, and Luigi lit cheap cigars to honor El Coco, exhaling clouds of stinky smoke that evaporated among the snowflakes.

"Who's next?" the cocinero asked.

"Not me," Luigi and I answered simultaneously.

"Gather ye rosebuds while ye may," Alfonso joked in English.

33. Duende

Aurelio Porta told me that Cathy Escudero had duende. "It's not something you can teach a person," he whispered into my ear at the dance studio. "You have to be born with it. And this girl is brimming over with duende. She's not conscious of it herself, she is so busy concentrating on the technical aspects of her craft. But the way she moves is like a gitana from Spain a thousand years old in her gypsy culture. She is like a ravishing murderess who loves to lick the blood off the knife afterwards. That is the magic of her art."

Aurelio had to lean very close to me when he said these things because Cathy's heels were battering the floorboards and Jorge was attacking the guitar in a controlled frenzy. They were electrifying. The dancer grabbed her skirt and swished it back and forth; she frowned and glowered and bit her tongue and grimaced. Her T-shirt was drenched under the armpits. Sometimes she yanked her dress up and down and we caught a flash of her cotton panties.

Aurelio never changed his tone of voice: "A champion racehorse has duende," he continued. "And Pelé possesses it, of course. Fangio had duende, and Manolete, too. And especially Gardel. Carlos Gardel had so much duende it caused his plane to hit another plane on the runway when he was only forty-eight. Gardel makes Frank Sinatra look like an amateur choirboy."

Jorge's fingers were a blur and Cathy was fast-stamping at the end of her alegrías. I was riveted by her performance, but Aurelio Porta never quit talking.

"Certain Americans have duende," he said. "Marlon Brando has it, and the late James Dean. Duende is an aberration in the soul. It is like a fire out of control. You don't see many old folks with duende—the force kills you early and you can't even stop yourself. You're not supposed to. All great artists are doomed. This chica is going to burn brightly for a short time and then the lightning inside will electrocute her. She will burst apart in flames. I hope I have a ticket to the performance because it will be horrible but exciting to watch. Duende is tragic, and when you see somebody who has it you must make the sign of the cross and spit in your palm. Duende is a curse. It makes people sacrifice themselves to give us pleasure. Duende is an enchanted living death for the person who has it."

He whispered these things loudly into my ear like a stockbroker giving quotations over the phone while Jorge and Cathy practiced to become famous and doomed. Outside on a gray afternoon random raindrops fell from the moody sky.

The studio was filled with thrilling music and frantic dancing. I fixated on Cathy's feet, then on Jorge's fingers. How could those two be so coordinated and exuberant?

"She has good footwork, but not great," Aurelio Porta said. "And technically she is competent but not too far above average. Yet that other thing, that fever, that instinct for presentation, that totally self-absorbed and self-destructive euphoria—that is special, that's duende. One in a million. She doesn't even know where it came from or how to control it. Like an erection in men. I can sell her, I know, even though she's not Spanish. I absolutely guarantee that she's going to be famous."

Jorge and Cathy stopped in unison with a bold and emotional flourish. Cathy held the pose for eight seconds until Aurelio Porta clapped, saying, "Bravo. Estupendo."

When Cathy knew she had been wonderful she became grumpy. "I stink," she muttered, panting, trying to catch her breath. "I dance like a wooden puppet. I have arthritis already and I'm not even twenty. Shit."

She went to her purse and extricated two cigarettes, handing one to Jorge. She rustled further seeking matches until Aurelio flipped over a book that skidded across the shiny floor, stopping at her feet. Kicking off her shoes, Cathy bent to retrieve the matches then leaned against the wall with her eyes closed, smiling. Jorge set the guitar flat on his lap and inhaled smoke luxuriously.

We savored the quiet. I was sweating as if I'd been dancing right along with Cathy Escudero.

"I'm going to retire when I'm twenty-five," she said. "By then I'll be a millionaire and a cripple."

Cathy slid down the mirror to a sitting position on the floor, hiking her dress up into her lap which gave us a glimpse of the white panties. Eyes closed, she seemed unaware of this fact.

Nobody said anything. Embarrassed, I averted my eyes, looking out a window. In the twilight most city lights had come on, but I could still see large foreboding clouds high above the Hudson River.

34. Handsome Anthony

Eduardo, Alfonso, and I attended a movie at the Waverly: *Il Bell'Antonio*. In Italian with English subtitles, it starred Marcello Mastroianni and Claudia Cardinale. It had been written by Pier Paolo Pasolini, one of Alfonso's heroes and the director of *Accatone!* Marcello played a handsome Sicilian rogue who fell in love with Claudia, the beautiful, virginal daughter of a town big shot. Despite his reputation as a womanizer, Marcello could not consummate the marriage. He had become impotent. This caused an enormous scandal. Marcello had failed Claudia, her parents, his own family, the church, the politicians, and all the rich businessmen of the city. Qué Vergüenza! Marcello's mother and father grew frantic. Claudia's parents demanded an annulment. Everyone was horrified that Marcello could not "be a man." Finally, Mastroianni admitted to his best friend that all his life he could easily screw prostitutes, shop girls, and casual affairs, but if he truly loved a woman he couldn't muster an erection.

When we left the theater, Eduardo said, "Fuck that movie. I hated that stupid film. Those Italians have their heads up their own rectums."

As we crossed Sixth Avenue, aiming for the empanada stand, Alfonso said, "Wait. Consider the dilemma. Pasolini was pointing out all the hypocrisy. It's an interesting story about how social mores, and especially religion, corrupt the nature of true love."

"Qué va!" Eduardo flung up his hands. "Marcello was a jerk. And why didn't Claudia help him out with a blowjob? That icy girl reminded me of Adriana."

"What do you think, blondie?" Alfonso asked.

"I felt sorry for Marcello," I answered. Truth is, the movie had terrified me.

At the empanada stand Roldán was talking sign language to the blue-haired amazon who knew Popeye—toothless Martha.

"Just my luck," she crowed. "The three most attractive studs in New York City."

Alfonso ordered coffee; Eduardo demanded a mate; I asked for a Coke. Martha sidled over to Eduardo, casting her arm around his shoulders.

"Whattayou say, big boy?"

Eduardo shook her off, rolling his eyes around. "No hablo inglés," he grumbled.

"He doesn't speak English," I lied.

She laughed. "Who cares what he doesn't speak? Language is not at issue here."

In Spanish Roldán asked, "How was the movie?"

Alfonso said, "Eduardo didn't like it."

"Why not?" The cook began washing stuff in his tiny sink.

"Because Claudia wouldn't give Marcello a blowjob."

"What are they talking about?" Martha asked me.

"It's all slang," I said. *Hello, déjà vu.* "I really don't understand a word."

35. See You Later, Alligator

I was prowling around the neighborhood at three A.M. when I bumped into Roldán and Santiago Chávez heading north past St. Anthony's Church on Sullivan Street. Inside the two cardboard boxes they carried were nestled tomorrow's empanadas. A tall, melancholy man, Santiago never visited the stand during commercial hours. But every night he helped the fat man cart the next day's product up to the kiosk.

Santiago ran a bakery hidden in his basement on Sullivan Street. You would never know it existed except for the wonderful odors seeping onto the sidewalk between midnight and five A.M. Roldán set his alarm for three each night so he could get up, walk south, and fetch his empanadas. Then he went back to sleep until noon.

Santiago made the pastelitos also. He didn't have a business license because it was cheaper to pay off the cops and the city inspectors.

I joined the two older men, relieving Roldán of his burden. With the cast on his arm it was harder for him to carry things.

"You came along just in time," he gasped. "I was getting tired. What are you doing up at this hour, blondie?"

"I'm always up at this hour," I said. "I'm a night owl, a murciélago, a vampire."

The cook laughed. "When I was young I used to stay up all night with my pals playing billiards or chasing women at the milongas. Believe it or not, I didn't used to be such a hippo."

Santiago never said a word. For a baker he sure was morose . . . and skinny.

We crossed West Houston which did not have a moving car visible in either direction. It always amazed me that Roldán could locomote at all. He walked sort of spread-legged and waddling like a penguin, puffing loudly, though he seemed pretty strong except when climbing stairs.

At the kiosk he removed a padlock and opened the door, squeezed into the alley, flipped a light switch, lifted the gate on the counter, and accepted one box from me and stashed it in the refrigerator. He took the other box from Santiago, who spun right around and retreated down the block to West Houston, returning to work.

Roldán handed me his portable TV so he could lock up. He'd forgotten it earlier. "I need television to sleep." I followed behind him on the stairs; we took a while to reach his apartment. His Christmas tree was still up, decorated by tinsel and a string of little lights. Half the needles had fallen off and been swept clean, but the lights were still blinking. I set the TV down on the kitchen table.

Roldán opened his refrigerator. "Do you need food, nene? What can I offer? Eggs? A carton of milk?"

I said, "No, no, I have plenty."

"Well, you should have a girl," the cocinero advised. "I worry about you. Late on a night like this they keep you warm in bed."

"Oh, I'll find one someday," I said.

"All you have to do is start talking to them." He closed the refrigerator door. "They don't care if it's nonsense. Every girl wants you to fuck her, I promise. It's biology."

I nodded and smiled brightly, embarrassed, trying to back away without being impolite. "I know," I said.

"No you don't. When a woman offers to buy you an empanada, you should accept and be grateful. She's making a play for you. It's an opportunity. Comprendés?"

"Sí. Comprendo."

Roldán must have felt that this was a rare moment alone and thus very important. He came over and grasped the door handle. "Listen," he said. "You're young and good-looking, blondie. There's a million fish in the ocean. It's easy if you just relax. Don't cripple yourself with fear or unreasonable expectations, okay?"

"Okay," I said, backing away some more, looking at my watch. "But I have to go now," I explained. "I'll see you later, alligator," I said in English, stepping over his threshold onto the landing.

Roldán began a fatherly gesture toward me but arrested it, searching my eyes, apologetic.

"After a while, crocodile," he replied, also in English—another expression that I had taught him.

Then he closed the door and I scampered downstairs to freedom.

36. Say "Cheese"

Aurelio Porta owned an expensive little camera and a tripod. He set up the tripod in the studio and took pictures of Cathy Escudero dancing. Sometimes he told Jorge to quit playing and ordered Cathy to freeze in a position so that he could expose it perfectly. The photographs would be used for publicity purposes. Cathy wore the blue flamenco dress she'd had on when I first met her last Halloween. It was robin's-egg blue with splashes of yellow flowers, and with lacy white hems of almost snowflake design at the sleeves, at the neckline, and at the bottom of the skirt. The dress transformed Cathy into an ethereal critter. She loved the effect of it and of the attention being paid to her by the camera.

After a while Aurelio told Jorge to cease playing altogether. It was better for Cathy to hold still in various poses even though that might sacrifice authenticity.

"There's nothing authentic about publicity pictures," he said. "You can't sell anything with the real deal."

"I *am* the real deal," Cathy said, holding her skirt out in a wide fan shape with one toe pointed down at the floor.

Aurelio scoffed, "That and a nickel will get you on the Staten Island Ferry."

"Jorge should be in the pictures." Cathy went and stood beside her guitarist with one arm around his shoulders. "Che, put out your cigarette. Assume the position. Look like a genius. And remove that hat, please."

She lifted the porkpie off Jorge's head but he grabbed it back. I had never seen his hair before. It was very dark, parted down the middle, and slicked flat against his head. He covered it up instantly with the hat.

Aurelio said, "We don't need any shots of the guitarist. This is about you, querida. You're the star. Guitarists are interchangeable."

Cathy reared up. "Jorge is *not* interchangeable. Without him I am nobody. We *belong* together."

Aurelio straightened behind the camera. He was a little miffed, but smiled.

"That's not the way it's done," he explained gently. "In a publicity photograph all attention must be placed on the central attraction. You never see a shot of Frank Sinatra with his pianist. You never see a picture of José Greco with his band. The band is great but anonymous because it's the dancer that our public has paid to see. The principal artist is everything."

Cathy pouted, then let it drop and began posing again. A moment later, though, she said, "I'm tired, that's enough." But she called over to me, "Dale, blondie. Come here. You too, Jorge. Let's get one photograph of the three of us together. I want a picture for my scrapbook."

I jumped up and was all set to walk over to her side when Aurelio Porta cut me off short.

"I'm sorry," he said, looking remorseful. "I can't do it. The camera is out of film."

"No it isn't," I said.

"Yes it is," he answered.

37. Thanks for Listening

Luigi and I helped lower the plywood shutter and set the padlocks, then we carried the portable TV and a crate of Cokes upstairs for the fat man. He invited us to stay and drink pisco while watching a late movie on TV. After five minutes Roldán fell asleep and began snoring. Luigi and I moved to the kitchen and killed half the pisco while Luigi never stopped talking. He told me about his old girlfriends Ana María, Esmerelda, and Carmen Ignacio; he described their physical attributes, their fashion habits, their ways of making love. Other girls he'd seduced and discarded were Sara, Isabel, Eva, and Mercedes. They had laughed when he tickled them; they had shouted gleefully during sex.

"Before my accident, girls were very simple for me," Luigi said. "Like picking flowers or gathering clamshells on the beach."

Now, of course, everything was different. "If I could have just one of those pibas back, any one, I would fall in love with her and stay that way forever."

I listened to him for an hour. Then I had to go home to work on my robber baron novel. Both of us were plastered.

"I'll come with you on the way to my place," Luigi said. He shrugged into his bomber jacket and lit another cigarette, then went to the spare bedroom and grabbed a few C-ration kits from a stack of cartons in the corner. "You want any, blondie? They're free."

"I thought the boss was marketing them for Popeye."

Luigi laughed. "You couldn't give this dung away to a seagull. But it'll keep you alive. Our large friend pays Popeye for at least five cartons a week. Then he gives it to desperadoes like me and Alfonso and Carlos the Artist and his wife who are starving to death."

I scooped up two kits, jamming them into my jacket pockets. Downstairs, the Figaro was closed for its Monday morning cleanup. Chairs were stacked on the tables and a sleepy boy wearing a grease-stained apron was mopping the floor.

As we traveled south on West Broadway, Luigi said, "The greatest problem for modern man is accepting his fate. I accept mine, yet no matter how often I labor to squash my former expectations they always crawl out of the grave and bite me. It's frustrating, but I don't believe in nihilism."

"What do you believe in?" I asked.

He stopped, glancing both ways as if checking for cops, then grabbed my arm and stared at me piercingly with those clear eyes trapped in his melted features.

"I believe in fucking," he said, "but I'm terrified that I'll die without ever getting laid again."

At the corner of West Broadway and Prince Street Luigi shook my hand, then he gripped both of my shoulders: "Thanks for listening, amigo. I bet you have problems also. How come you never tell us about them, blondie? Next time it's your turn, okay?"

"Okay," I said.

38. Escape from Freedom

Rain fell steadily on Greenwich Village.

I was sitting alone in Figaro's reading a dog-eared copy of *Escape from Freedom* by Erich Fromm that Alfonso had forced on me. I looked up when La Petisa shed her raincoat and sat down opposite me, saying in English, "Hello, blondie, how are they hanging today?"

Her sudden arrival caught me by surprise. She had on too much makeup but looked cute in her green Swiss hat, a crewneck sweater with an overlapped Peter Pan collar, black slacks, and red rubber boots. I haven't mentioned this, but she worked uptown at an Argentine travel agency.

"I'm okay," I said. "How are you?"

"Happy as a clam," she acknowledged, still in English. "I found myself a tiny sublet in Flushing. It's great to be independent again. I don't like depending on the kindness of strangers. What are you reading?"

I showed her the book. "Alfonso insists. He thinks all Americans are philistines."

"Alfonso thinks his own *mother* is a philistine." She snapped her fingers for the attractive blonde waitress from Boston. "I'll have a cappuccino. And how about you, blondie? Would you like another hot chocolate? On me. I'm a poor little rich girl swimming in dollars and cents."

"I'm okay. Thanks anyway."

She said abruptly, "Why are you so *passive,* man? What are you *afraid* of?"

"I'm not afraid of anything," I lied. "I'm just quiet, I guess. I'm sorry."

"Okay, where do you live?" she asked, chipper again. "I don't know anything about you. What kind of apartment is it? Why don't you invite me over for a cup of tea? I won't hurt you. I'm harmless. I'm just curious, that's all. You're so subdued at the empanada stand I don't even know how well you understand Spanish."

"I miss a lot of words but I understand okay," I said. "Where's Popeye?"

"He's history already. Mr. Casanova couldn't stop sneaking out to bang this toothless whale in a blue wig, so I said, 'Hasta luego.' Of course, the minute I did, Eduardo tried to jump my bones. But no thank you. He gives me the creeps because he's a cuckold. Thank goodness he went last week to shoot a documentary film about voodoo in Haiti."

I said, "I'm amazed at all the stuff that happens to our gang."

She leaned forward. "So tell me, blondie. Why do you hang out at the kiosk anyway? Do you yearn for a Latin soul?"

That made me laugh. I said, "Yes."

She laughed too. "You're our little gringo mascot, aren't you? Is your apartment far away? Cheers." She clacked her cappuccino cup against my empty hot chocolate mug. "Here's lookin' at you, kid."

I said, "I've never heard you speak English like this before."

"That's because we're always with the illiterates, excluding Alfonso, of course. Do you have a girlfriend, blondie? I heard rumors about a flamenco dancer. Would you like to attend a movie sometime? How about *West Side Story* or *The Misfits*?"

"With you?"

La Petisa glanced right and left. "No. I was thinking maybe with the long-haired dope over there wearing that macramé rug around her shoulders."

"I don't know. I work every night on my writing. Ever since I got laid off at the Night Owl I've been dead broke."

"I already told you, I have money. What are you writing about?"

"Just different things. Short stories and a couple of novels." Why had I opened my mouth?

"I wrote a novel once," she said. "It was about all my different novios. And my cat was in it. I used to have a wonderful cat. His name was Trueno."

She clicked open her purse, taking out a note pad displaying the travel agency logo, and pushed the pad over to me. "Write down your phone number, okay? I'll give you a call sometime."

"I don't have a telephone," I said.

"Okay. Write down your address and I'll stop by on a Saturday if you want. We could go to a museum. Have you ever seen the Degas ballerinas at the Metropolitan?"

Signing my own death warrant, I carefully printed my address and pushed the pad back to her. She returned it to her purse without looking, then checked her wristwatch. Standing abruptly, she put on the raincoat.

"Sorry to rush, kiddo. I have an appointment now. You can finish my cappuccino. Don't worry, I don't have cooties."

Then she leaned over and tapped *Escape from Freedom*. "Tell Alfonso that Erich Fromm is full of shit. Too much thinking spoils the broth. Fair enough?"

"If you say so," I said, and she winked at me.

39. Coffee with Jorge

You could see what was happening between Cathy Escudero and Aurelio Porta, but I went to the dance studio anyway. It felt bad, yet I couldn't stop myself. Cathy liked an audience because it made her dance more intensely. I had memorized a half dozen of her flamenco routines and I could play them over in my head whenever I took a break from writing or if I was lying in bed unable to sleep. I knew every move of bulerías and all the llamadas. I could picture each graceful sequence defining the tientos introduction of her tango. Whenever I pictured Cathy dancing, I heard Jorge on the guitar. Together they were a great team.

Other people came to the practices. A white-haired guy outfitted in a black turtleneck jersey was a friend of Aurelio's and seemed like the archetypal Latin gigolo. An austere woman, probably late fifties, stood against the wall smoking cigarettes—her expression never changed. She wore a tweed jacket and slacks and pointy cowboy boots.

After one session the two new people went off with Cathy and Aurelio in a taxi, leaving Jorge and me on the sidewalk high and dry in windy April weather.

I recovered first, asking, "Querés un cafecito?"

"Sí."

We walked over to the Downtown Café. At that hour of the afternoon it was almost deserted. We selected a booth and Jorge lit right up, offering me a cigarette I refused.

"You really play well," I said. It was the first time I'd given him a compliment. Unlike Cathy, he never asked for one and usually remained so distant that I rarely addressed him directly.

Jorge shrugged and smoked his cigarette facing out the window.

"Do you play for other dancers?" I asked.

"No. Only for Catalina. I'm not good enough yet."

I said, "I think you are wonderful."

He shrugged again. "That's because you don't understand flamenco. I'm way down at the bottom of the ladder."

"I think you're at the top."

Jorge glanced at me disdainfully. "I have a lot to learn," he said in a tone that suggested we should drop it.

"Do you go to school?" I asked.

"No. I practice."

"How many hours a day?"

"Maybe eight or ten."

"Don't your fingers wear out?"

He cocked his head and frowned as the tone of his voice changed completely. "If the soul is on fire the body never gets tired."

Our usual waitress had pretty green eyes and an attractive smile. She joked, "Howdy, boys. What'll it be today? Two piña coladas with fresh shredded coconut and maraschino cherries?"

I said, "Yes, plus a black coffee, please."

Jorge told me to ask her for coffee also. He had been a New Yorker for a year but was unable to speak one word of English, or to understand the simplest statement or interrogative in that language. He didn't like talking to gringos, he was afraid of them. He wanted to keep himself purely Spanish for his art. Cathy had told me that Jorge was illiterate in his own language and could not read a note of music.

"All musicians are idiots," Alfonso once said. "The genius ones can't even count to ten. I knew an Argentine guy with a lobotomy who could play the violin like a lost soul from paradise. You can shoot a true musician between the eyes and he won't even blink."

Without Cathy as a buffer between me and Jorge I felt uncomfortable just as I had with Roldán at Thanksgiving. Jorge had no interest in asking about my life. He'd always tolerated my quirky Spanish, but now he grew impatient with my slow phrasing and butchered grammar.

We finished our coffee and went out onto the sidewalk. Jorge carried his guitar case and had a fresh cigarette in his mouth. He had big ears and looked very childish under the porkpie hat. I shook his hand: "Adiós, muchacho—*ciao.*" He nodded and walked away, holding himself proudly and moving between pedestrians with confident arrogance. I had a longing to run after him and say something else, but how could I do that without triggering his scorn?

40. Cataclysms

By myself I went to another screening of *Jules and Jim,*
the movie by François Truffaut. Maybe it would give me
even more insights than it had the first time. So much had
happened since then. I tried to pay attention to every move
the characters made and to the words they spoke in French,
which had English subtitles. I yearned for Jeanne Moreau
the same way I yearned for Cathy Escudero. Moreau was
so attractive, seductive, dangerous, and volatile. Jules and
Jim were friends like Alfonso and myself. Jules was Austrian,
Jim was French. Aurelio Porta was like the movie interloper,
Albert, who, after being wounded in the First World War,
consummated an affair with Jeanne Moreau, whose name in
the movie was Catherine, another omen. Catherine was
married to Jules and they had a daughter, Sabine. The
story was very complicated. Catherine fell in love with Jim,
Jules's best friend. Sort of. She also had affairs with other
men because she was tired of being married to Jules. Jules
was desperately in love with Catherine. Jules and Jim loved
each other, and Jim also loved a girl named Gilberte. Gilberte could be compared to my friend Alfonso's patient lover,
Sofía. Jim slept with other women, yet his principal girl was
Gilberte, who suffered deeply when Jim became obsessed by
Catherine. In the end, Jules, who seemed to be the weakest
member of the trio that included Jim and Catherine, was the
only one who survived.

The heart has its reasons which even reason does not
understand. I thought about Alfonso's two novias, Renata
and Sofía. I thought about La Petisa with Gino, then with

Luigi, then with Popeye. And then she had flirted with me— why me? I thought about Eduardo and Adriana, and I also thought about all of the girlfriends Luigi had before his face got burned. I thought of Chuy's book of girls and his attitude toward women, and I wondered why girls were attracted to cripples. I didn't forget Roldán and Teresa Mono, the girl who broke his heart and exiled him from Argentina. Nor did I forget Popeye and Martha, or Gino's surprise that I didn't have a girlfriend: *Che, blondie, all you need is* this.

In the movie, Jules said, "All these hearts reaching out toward each other, my God what pain they cause." Jeanne Moreau was also like Alfonso's girl Renata—mercurial. Above all she wanted her way and her freedom. Jules was like me, and also like Alfonso's other girl, Sofía, who resembled Jim's patient long-suffering lover, Gilberte. How could Cathy Escudero be attracted to a man like Aurelio Porta?

I sat through the next showing of the movie. There was a moment in Paris, seconds before Catherine jumped into the Seine, where Jim and Jules quoted Baudelaire on the subject of women. Baudelaire said they were "abominable," "monsters," "assassins of art," "little fools," "little sluts," "imbecilic," and "depraved." He added, "I have always been astonished that women are allowed in churches. What can they have to say to God?"

When Jim and Catherine finally made love, Jim became emotionally enslaved to her and all other women ceased to exist for him. Jules accepted the loss of his wife and remained friends with Jim in order to stay as close as possible to Catherine. Soon Catherine became jealous of Jim, they parted, then they got back together, but parted again, and Jim was finally planning to marry Gilberte when Catherine reappeared and lured Jim back to her, and their story ended in tragedy.

At another crucial point of the film Jules explained Catherine to Jim. "She is a force of nature," he said. "She describes herself in cataclysms."

I left the theater all tuckered out and wanting to describe myself in cataclysms.

41. A Brand-New Hand

Chuy's arm had been fitted with a new hand and he swung by the kiosk to show it off. Alfonso, Luigi, myself, and the fat man were his audience. The friendly weather had us feeling peppy. Maybe spring had turned the corner? Luigi had won $230 betting on the trotters last night. He was overjoyed to hear that La Petisa had already dropped that scoundrel Popeye. Alfonso had just showed us a German mathematics magazine in which he had published two articles. He said the math was boring but pointed out several hilarious puns he'd inserted into the text. Roldán held up his cast, stating that he would never remove it because so many people had inscribed the white plaster of Paris with poetry and drawings. It was a work of art.

Chuy had a black glove over his new hand and the prosthetic looked almost real.

"I'll learn how to caress women with it. I expect to double my volume of dates. I've already started taking vitamins. Watch how I can choose which finger to wiggle."

"It's a dead hand," Alfonso said. "You can't really feel with it."

Chuy disagreed. "No, it's a miracle of modern medicine. The best hand money can buy."

"But all the same a dead hand," Alfonso reiterated. "Some people could invest that hand with feeling, but for you it will only be a pornographic crab claw that scuttles and grabs and grasps."

Chuy warned him to stop casting aspersions. "I don't want to hurt you."

Luigi said, "Profe is right. What woman wants to be touched by your wooden fingers?"

Chuy, astonished, couldn't believe who was talking. "Shut your mouth you perverted disciple of Onan."

Roldán tactfully shifted the focus. "Hey, manco, will you take off the hand when you go swimming?"

"I don't know." Chuy seemed puzzled. "I hadn't thought of that. And you, profe, and you, quemado: When was the last time you guys did it to a piba, ten years ago?"

Alfonso ignored him but delivered a brief dissertation to the rest of us. "The feeling in a hand comes from the heart. Some men and women, even if they lost their hands, would have wooden prosthetics capable of touching with as much sensitivity as most flesh appendages. But not Chuy. That new hand is a piece of wood full of Novocain."

"You're joking," Chuy said.

"No. I am dead serious."

"You're jealous because even with two hands you can't get a woman. You're a shriveled-up pipsqueak with no virility or charisma, old before your time."

"Oh shut up," Luigi said. "You are a miserable pimp."

"For creeps like you desperate for my services."

"Your *funeral* services." Alfonso extended his coffee cup for a free refill. "I can't stand morbid sex freaks."

"Okay." Chuy put up his dukes. "You went too far that time, profe."

Luigi cried, "Mirá, che! Don't break your new hand. Think of the money involved."

Chuy stopped. "Oops, I hadn't thought of that. This thing cost me an arm and a leg." Then he checked his watch. "Hah.

In fifteen minutes I'll be getting the old do-si-do from a chick who has a pair of thirty-eight-inch pechugas. Gentlemen, synchronize your watches. And think of me then."

Briskly he strode away, heading west.

Fifteen minutes later Roldán looked at his watch and said, "Another round of coffee gratis to honor that jackal." He dropped two pies into the grease bin for a Jersey tourist.

As we sipped the steaming liquid Alfonso said, "Someday he'll catch a disease and we can all kiss him good-bye."

Luigi said, "I hate that wooden hand more than I hate my own face."

I said, "He's not all bad. He paid for El Coco's cremation."

The boss glanced at his watch again. "He is probably through now, my friends."

"He's making notations in his book," Alfonso grumbled.

Luigi said, "Now she's putting on fresh lipstick so he can take a picture for his God damn portfolio."

They fell silent. Nobody said a word. The empanadas sizzled.

Finally, Roldán laughed. He said, "You boys look like camel shit in the zoo."

42. Epiphany

Cathy couldn't get into it. Jorge kept stopping when he made a mistake and starting over. He made a lot of mistakes. He couldn't concentrate. Then Cathy made a mistake and stopped and clenched her fists and stamped her foot angrily.

Aurelio Porta said, "Hey, hey, relax, nenes. You accomplish nothing with undisciplined anger. Perfection is all about the control of emotional chaos."

He was standing against the wall beside another of his pals, a diminutive gangster wearing a hairpiece and a double-breasted suit who removed his smokes from a slim, sterling silver box.

Jorge lit a cigarette and faced out the window in the other direction. Cathy threw up her hands but said nothing. She circled around, frowning and counting under her breath, trying to remember the tricky sequence of beats and visualize in her head all her body moves and the footwork also. Aurelio Porta folded his arms, watching her.

Jorge smoked the cigarette down to a short butt and flicked it through the open window, still lit.

The Uruguayan chuckled and said to me, "Temperamental artists." He shrugged. *What can you do?*

Cathy asked Jorge, "What's the matter?"

"Nada."

"Okay, let's try again. Okay?"

"De acuerdo."

Jorge formed the fingers of his left hand into an A chord, tapped his right toe three times, and began playing. Aurelio began doing his palmas, clapping softly in rhythm. And Cathy danced her little heart out but they continued goofing up and having to start over. It wasn't pretty. Aurelio Porta tried to spur them on by clapping louder. He also grimaced and glanced at his watch a couple of times. Once again he looked over at me and said, "These things happen." Another shrug. *What the hell.*

The double-breasted toupee beside him never said a word.

I wanted to leave early but didn't. Cathy appeared clumsy and Jorge was out of his element. I did not understand the problem.

At one point Cathy stood still in the middle of the studio with her head tilted back and her arms hanging limply. She inhaled a deep breath and exhaled. Jorge slumped over his guitar and lit another cigarette. I stood up and stretched. Nobody said anything.

When Cathy lowered her head and stared at me I realized her face wasn't just sweaty, she had been crying. She bit her lip. She seemed befuddled.

Then she turned to Jorge and said, "All right, you son of a bitch, this time let's *do* it."

And suddenly they created an epiphany together. They entered another realm that was sublime and diabolical. They soared, never making an error, and their flawless execution even made Aurelio Porta shut up.

All art yearns for bliss. Aurelio quit doing his palmas. I resisted the urge to blink as the rapture intensified between the guitarist and his dancer. I wanted to avert my eyes from their vehemence.

How can it be explained? Jorge abandoned his reserve completely to become a ferocious man. And Cathy kowtowed to his staccato melodies like an erotic slave girl precisely obedient to her musician. What a shocking reversal of power—the peon as brutal master. Jorge drove Cathy relentlessly. It was raw and beautiful.

Aurelio Porta didn't like it. I was startled. The performance was more than wonderful, it was scary. When they abruptly stopped I let out a small cry. Jorge shut his eyes triumphantly and Cathy held her dramatic finishing pose as if pinioned by a sharp dagger against the wall.

Aurelio broke the hush. "That wasn't bad," he said in English.

To Jorge, in Spanish, Cathy reiterated, "He says that wasn't bad."

Aurelio added in Spanish, "But you were both too shrill, without any nuance at all. You kill all the emotion when you stay at fever pitch straight through."

Jorge opened his eyes. They were dark, drugged and threatening, like a murderer's. Then he wilted, becoming a stupid boy again, casual and impervious.

43. Six Roses

Presto!

Finally the weather had changed for good. Roldán set a blossoming daffodil in a pot on the window ledge of the empanada stand. The flower declared: *Relax. Winter is over.* You could feel enthusiasm and germination on the air. Across the street Dante's Café had put two little tables and four chairs on the sidewalk.

Popeye said, "I heard you had a crush on that flamenco dancer from Buenos Aires who thinks she's a Spaniard from Andalucía. Is it true, blondie?"

I shook my head. "Not true. You heard incorrectly."

Gino was running the empanada stand because Roldán had retired early after selling a hundred pies and ten gallons of coffee. Tourists had been by in droves celebrating spring, but now they were tapering off.

Popeye offered me a bite of his chicken empanada, which I accepted.

He said, "If you're interested in a piba, you have to pay her a lot of attention. Women don't simply fall into your arms out of the sky. They want to be appreciated before they'll give you a peek at the beaver. The best way to start is with flowers."

He produced his wallet, removing two one-dollar bills that he placed on the counter beside my coffee cup.

"Here you go, kid. There's a flower shop up on Eighth Street next to Sam Kramer's jewelry store. You should buy six roses. They will be your ticket to the Promised Land."

I shook my head and smiled. "Thank you, but I can't take the money. I don't need six roses."

"Every man needs six roses," Popeye said. "Even a guy like me once in a while. I gave La Petisa twelve roses but she dropped me anyway because she wanted orchids instead. Pussy is more fickle than a prince with a glass slipper."

Then he snatched back his money before I could change my mind.

Poof! Eduardo's ex-wife, Adriana, materialized just like a rabbit produced from a hat. She had on a yellow shirtwaist dress that seemed cheerful and way out of character.

"Where's Luigi?" she asked. "Have any of you boys seen him?"

Popeye pointed east: "He's at Roosevelt Raceway betting on the trotters."

"Why? Who wants to know?" Gino said.

But Adriana had already dematerialized with another magical whoosh.

A minute later Alfonso arrived at the stand fit to be tied. He had a typed, four-page letter from Renata. Holding up the scented epistle in one fist, he slapped it with his other hand.

"Look at *this*!" he cried. "*Listen* to what I have to put up with!"

He started reading out loud. "'What is the matter with you, my darling? You crave me, I crave you, you are wonderful, I am wonderful, why do you refuse to admit it? The United States is destroying your brain, honey, blasting it apart with gringo tonterías. You're a genius and genius needs the support of a woman like *me*. Do you have another novia in New York? I hope she gives you syphilis and a brain tumor. Sweetheart, think of my lips playing your little flute. Don't you miss my beautiful tits? Are you eating properly? How can you be so cruel to the woman you love?'"

He stopped. "It goes on and on. She badgers, she cajoles, she quotes poetry by Shakespeare and Lord Byron. She keeps threatening to kiss the jerk she's dating but I think Renata just invented him to torment me. Y mirá, she even puts her red lipstick print across all the margins."

He thrust the pages toward us so we could see.

Gino said, "Tell her to fuck off. I wouldn't put up with that."

He untied his apron because it had a grease spot and took a clean apron from a pile under the counter. Gino was fastidious about protecting his custom shirts, his pleated trousers, his perforated wingtips.

"But she's so *beautiful*," Alfonso said. "She has strawberry blonde hair and large hazel eyes. Her voice is husky and seductive. She looks like Rita Hayworth."

Gino was not impressed. "It doesn't matter what she looks like. She's breaking your balls."

I said, "And your other girl, Sofía, is such a good person. She's so gentle and considerate."

Alfonso groaned, "Who *cares*? Sofía is not *radiant*. She's not like Ingrid Bergman in *Casablanca*."

A bouncy blonde wearing a navy pea jacket showed up at the window obviously enamored of Gino, who told us later that Simone was a French au pair from Marseilles living with a rich family on Fifth Avenue. She spoke rudimentary Spanish enhanced by an adorable French accent and only stayed long enough to make a date with Gino. Then she dashed off tickled pink by her own audacity.

Gino remarked casually that behind closed doors Simone was "a *very* sexy girl."

I went home and wrote a short story about a guy who was half Gino, half Aurelio Porta. In the story my protagonist conquered innumerable beauties from several continents, including a dead ringer for Cathy Escudero.

Then he caught syphilis and died of a brain tumor.

44. Cherry Pie

My fourth-choice publisher rejected the college romance without comment. *Damn.* I picked up the manuscript and walked it south to the next guys on my list. Then I headed for the dance studio feeling uncomfortable and constrained. I entered the building and went up in the elevator and walked down the corridor to the studio. The door was slightly ajar and I could hear the guitar and Cathy's heels banging out rhythms. I hesitated, not even peeking inside, and took a stance against the wall on the hinged side of the door, listening.

I could imagine every step and every gesture. I could see the stern expression on Jorge's face and the way he held the guitar rigidly and high, his features indifferent as his fingers did all the work. I also knew that Aurelio Porta was in attendance watching and keeping score.

I stood in the corridor with my arms folded for about five minutes listening to their practice session. When they took a breather I walked away quickly, using the stairs instead of the elevator. I hurried east on Fourteenth Street to the Downtown Café. The green-eyed waitress came to my booth saying, "Hi, where are your buddies?" She whisked a pencil from her hair above the ear and poised the tip against an order pad.

"It's early. They're still at practice."

The waitress glanced around, then slipped onto the padded bench across the table from me and lit a cigarette. She had a few freckles and her lips were shaped in an attractive little pout.

"I'm bushed," she said. "My feet are killing me. I wish I could inherit a million dollars and move to Las Vegas and live in a mansion with a swimming pool."

After three quick puffs she stubbed out the cigarette but kept on talking.

"My boyfriend got arrested yesterday. He has the brains of a Lincoln Log. He works in a gas station and stole two tires and sold them to another guy for half price. The boss found out because Bobby left his cap on the rack he took the tires off of. So now he's on Rikers Island and I'm supposed to pay the rent with tips I get in this joint? Good luck. What's your story?"

I said, "I don't know. I don't have a story."

"Everybody has a story." She smiled sympathetically. "I see you in here how many times over the last few months— maybe a dozen? First you're only with that spiffy little girl and the skinny guy in the weird hat with the guitar case. I bet she's a dancer; I bet you're in love with her; and I bet she won't give you the time of day. Am I close?"

"I don't know. Maybe a little bit."

"The kid with the guitar, he's her brother?"

"No. He's from Spain. She's from Buenos Aires."

"Where is Baynose Iris?"

"In Argentina. At the bottom of the world. Near Antarctica."

"You mean in South America?"

"Yes."

"Okay. The kid from Spain is in love with her also. You guys are a triangle."

I laughed. "I don't think so. She's older than him by a lot. She never flirts with him. He's very quiet."

"Quiet waters run deep," she said. "But anyway, one day you all appear with an older guy, the Latin playboy with

Liberace hair. At first I think he could be the father, but he's all over her like a rug while you two guys sit there twiddling your thumbs. The plot thickens, am I correct?"

I was surprised. I said, "You sure notice a lot, don't you?"

She chuckled. "I'm a trained professional." Then she flinched. "Oops. The wicked witch just shot me an eyeball, I better take your order." She popped up and took out her pad. "So what'll it be?"

"I guess I want a coffee," I said. "No cream or sugar."

"How about with a slice of cherry pie on the side? Live it up."

"I don't have the plata," I admitted.

"The what?"

"The money."

"It's on me," she said, scribbling down the order. "I'll steal it for you."

Before I could protest she was gone. After a minute she returned with the coffee and the pie.

"Here you go, sir, one slice of pie and a cup of coffee just like God created it, black, no frills. Ain't it beautiful?"

She set them down and tore the check off her pad and placed it facedown beside the pie plate. Then off she went to clear another table.

When I turned over the check I saw that she had only charged me for the coffee and had written *Cheer up!* on top.

Was she making a play for me?

45. Why So Glum?

I filched a newspaper from a Washington Square trash basket and sat on a bench to read it. Everybody was nervous about confrontations between the East and the West. A long article explained how to evacuate New York in case of attack. I folded the paper and put it back in the wastebasket.

Then I sat quietly on the bench wondering if I would be drafted. I didn't want to invade the Soviet Union or wear a radiation suit for cleanup duty after a bomb blast. I simply wanted to publish my college novel and marry Cathy Escudero.

The park was filled with people having a good time on a warm day. Kids and young adults splashed through the fountain. A Good Humor cart was back. Up in the trees two squirrels leaped from branch to branch, chasing each other. I felt burdened by anxiety.

Alfonso sat down beside me, clapping his hand on my shoulder. "Hello, blondie, why so glum? On a day like this you should be joyful."

"I don't want to be drafted and die before I publish a novel," I said. Immediately I wished I hadn't said that.

Alfonso placed his arm around my shoulder and squeezed. "You won't die, nene. I promise."

"How do you know?"

He said, "Humanity is crazy, but not that crazy. No species that created Shakespeare, Mozart, Picasso, and Marilyn Monroe could ever destroy itself. I promise."

I replied, "But the same species created Hitler, Mussolini, and Jack the Ripper."

He scoffed, "Those jerks were canceled out long ago by Gina Lollobrigida and Sophia Loren."

"What about Stalin and Tojo?" I asked.

He retorted while cleaning his glasses on a filthy handkerchief: "They are easily trumped by Tolstoy, Borges, Dickens, and Neruda."

"Okay. You win, profe. I give up. Let's go to a movie."

"There's a Jacques Tati film at the New School, blondie."

So that's where we went. And the movie was zany and delightful and it really cheered me up.

46. Cheating

Tennis racket in hand, I went to the playground on Thompson Street between Prince and Spring. I had on Bermuda shorts and a torn old polo shirt. Ah, sweet primavera: The sun was bright as a bulb. For an hour I hit a ball against the high wall designed for handball games. Nearby stood two basketball hoops and a bocce court where old men from Palermo and Bari were joking with one another. A high chain-link fence surrounded the area.

I was exercising all alone when Carlos the Artist walked past nursing a coffee-to-go he'd purchased at Miguel's All-Nite Puerto Rican Deli on Spring Street. Surprised to see me, he stopped and peered through the fence.

"Look, if it isn't Rod Laver in person. Cómo estás, blondie?"

I grabbed the tennis ball and waved. "I'm great. Thanks."

"Che, vení." Carlos motioned me over. "I want to speak with you."

I walked closer and we talked through the fence. He had on black motorcycle boots, black chinos, a Snoopy T-shirt, and a red baseball cap that said CCCP. He had dyed his mustache purple.

"You look like a pro, blondie, whacking that pelota. Where did you learn, in school?"

I told him yes. He said he had always wanted to play tennis, but the only sport he'd ever excelled at was fucking. Speaking of which, now that fate had thrust us together, he had another favor to ask of me.

"Sure. You can use my apartment anytime, amigo. Tell me when and I'll leave the key with Roldán."

"No, I don't want your apartment. It's about my wife."

"Your wife?"

"I want you to screw her, blondie. You can even kiss her if you want."

"*What?*"

"Oíme." He took another sip of coffee, then leaned closer to the fence. "It would be a favor to both of us. She's bored, I'm bored, we both need a little boost to get the adrenaline going. You know what I mean?"

No I didn't. "Talk slower, por favor."

"Don't be an ignoramus, friend. You understand very well. You're a man. Aren't you a man?"

I nodded yes, I was a man.

"So it's simple," he said. "I know where you live. We'll make a date and I'll bring her by. You two will have fun, she's very affectionate. When it's over just grab her a cab on West Broadway. I'll make sure she has the guita."

I stalled. "I'm sorry. What are you talking about?"

Carlos looked exasperated. After glancing both ways, he leaned closer to the fence and fixed his big eyes on me.

"Listen carefully, friend. I've got a deeper problem with my wife. She's pissed off at me. This country makes them goofy. Sure I play around, I screw the minas when I want, it's my right. Back home nobody gives a damn. It's normal behavior. But up here it's called 'cheating,' and the wives get in a twit about it. And even if you're a foreigner the local culture rubs off eventually. So now my wife is not only bored but she wants revenge. And who would be more perfect for her revenge than you? Then maybe she'll quit bugging me."

I squinted my eyes, grimacing, and said, "But I don't even know your wife's name."

"It's Esther. She was born in Chile. Her screwball mom admired that North American movie actress who always wore a bathing suit."

"But she's your *wife*," I said.

Carlos rolled his eyes, then tried to hide his exasperation by speaking very slowly and very clearly, as if to a child.

"Hey. Just for now suspend your prejudices. I'm giving you a college education on the psychology of sex. I told you my wife is bored. I'm bored too. You can't just bang the same person forever and keep it interesting. So this will stir things up, killing a couple of birds with one stone. For starters, it'll make me jealous, blondie. It will give her an illicit thrill and more sexual confidence as well as revenge. I'll be angry at her for 'cheating' on me. She'll get enraged at me for forcing her to 'cheat' with you. Sounds bad, but ultimately anger and jealousy mixed together are a fabulous aphrodisiac. Do you see what I'm driving at? You may think it's complicated, but it's really very simple."

I said, "You should ask Chuy. He'll know what to do in this situation."

"Chuy? Are you *kidding* me? If Chuy ever even *looks* at my wife I'll hire Gino to break all his bones."

"Well, maybe Gino is your guy, then. He really understands the pibas."

Carlos drained his coffee, crumpled the cup, and tossed it on the sidewalk.

"What am I, *crazy*? Gino is handsome, he has no principles, he's a varón. I want to *stimulate* my wife, I don't want to *lose* her."

I blurted, "*But I don't want to fuck your wife!*"

Carlos eyed me with suspicion, then he realized I was sincere and shrugged wistfully in defeat. "Bueno. So be it. I knew it was a long shot, but no harm done, correct? Don't ever tell anybody about this, okay?"

"Okay," I promised.

Carlos laughed, pointing his finger at me like a little pistol. Then he said, "Pop!" and proceeded along the sidewalk in an easterly direction.

47. ¿Qué Hora Es?

When I opened the dance studio door Jorge was sitting in his chair smoking a cigarette with the guitar on his lap, awaiting Cathy. The windows were open; the air smelled fresh and tangy. When Jorge exhaled, breezes blew the smoke in various directions.

"Where is Cathy?" I asked him.

Jorge shrugged. "No sé."

I didn't see her dance bag or sneakers lying nearby. Jorge was alone and had been that way for a while. I checked my watch; I was late. They already should have been practicing for twenty minutes. Jorge wore his porkpie hat, a white T-shirt, and baggy pleated brown slacks without cuffs from Spain. Though old and cracked, his shoes were polished spic-and-span. His cigarette pack and book of matches lay on the sooty window ledge.

I claimed my usual spot, asking him, "Did she say she would be late?"

He shrugged again and sucked on his cigarette. Something was wrong. Aurelio Porta wasn't there, nor were any of his cronies. Jorge seemed calm and unconcerned.

"Has she ever been late like this?"

Jorge shook his head. "Nunca."

"I wonder what happened?"

He shrugged once more, then leaned down and snuffed the cigarette with his shoe, then picked up the butt and snapped it out the window.

"There's a telephone downstairs on the sidewalk." I searched my pockets for a dime. "We could call her and see what's up."

He waggled his finger back and forth. "No tiene teléfono."

Jorge lit another cigarette, politely gesturing the pack toward me so I could raise my hand to decline his invitation. He appeared to be really skinny in the T-shirt and baggy trousers. I wondered if he had enough money to eat okay and if smoking had damaged his lungs. His skin was pallid. He didn't look so tough.

Jorge tapped his wrist asking silently, *Qué hora es?* I told him. He nodded and blew a smoke ring. Way crosstown, police sirens whooped. Below us cars and buses accelerated, honking impatiently. One of Jorge's fingers touched a chord by mistake, releasing a clear little twang.

I said, "Well, do you want to play something while we wait?"

He regarded me as if I was crazy.

"Did Aurelio or any of his friends drop by?"

Jorge smiled. He said, "No." I don't know if I'd ever seen him smile. There was a gap between his front teeth. He looked vulnerable, especially with those big ears under the brim of his porkpie hat. I had never seen the hat off except the one time Cathy grabbed it.

We sat still for another ten minutes waiting for Cathy Escudero. Jorge bent over to place the guitar in its case, then tapped his wrist again asking for the time. After that he sat immobile, arms folded, head tilted slightly, eyes closed. I stared out the windows feeling nervous. Pigeons perched along a parapet across the street were cooing.

I said, "She isn't going to come, is she?"

Jorge smiled again, his face lighting up, very incongruous.

"How long are we going to wait?" I asked.

"No sé." He took out an emery board and began filing his nails, shaping them carefully. He was pretending to be bored.

At six o'clock five young girls wearing toe shoes, blue stretch tights, and knitted leg warmers arrived to take over our space. Their lanky teacher asked, "Where's the flamenco hotshot?"

"We don't know," I said. "Maybe sick or kidnapped."

The teacher said, "You can't get sick if you're a dancer. Somebody else will take your place."

Jorge picked up his guitar case, nodded good-bye to me, and left the room. I hastened to catch up and walked alongside of him.

"I hope she isn't sick," I said.

"She's not sick," he answered.

48. Off to Mexico

Popeye, Chuy, and Luigi were going to Mexico City on Thursday for the first bullfights of spring. Popeye double-parked the diaper truck nearby and hopped out accompanied by Luigi. The sailor and the burnt man were pals again and La Petisa could go screw herself.

Luigi said, "The diaper truck will be our conveyance. Who else wants to come along?"

Gino eyed the truck dubiously. "That cacharro will never make it."

Popeye was offended. "My truck? You jest."

"They won't let it into Mexico," Gino assured him. "It's a wreck. Once in, you'd never get it out."

"Chuy promised to buy tires and tune the engine. He'll pay the gas. We are going to sleep on mattresses in back. Chuy might bring two girls."

Everybody, including Roldán, left the stand to inspect the truck. Three mattresses were laid out sideways in back with assorted blankets piled on top of them.

"When is the first corrida?" I asked.

"Two weeks from Sunday," said Luigi.

"There will be warm weather and mariachis." Popeye's face glowed. "We're only stopping by to see who else is interested."

Not Alfonso. "I have exams. I need to study. I'm pretending to be a grown-up."

Luigi said, "In Mexico City I am going to see the Rivera and Orozco and Siqueiros murals, and also Trotsky's tomb. Then I'm going to hump my brains out with cheap hookers who will have to look at my face because I'm paying them."

Popeye turned to me. "How about it, blondie? I have a compañero in D.F. who can get us marijuana and we'll go for a ride across the floating gardens of Xochimilco."

I hemmed a little. "I don't know . . . I'm working hard . . . I don't have money . . ."

What I meant was I couldn't go to Mexico because I had to open my mailbox each day in case there was a postcard asking me to pick up my novel because it had been rejected again.

Roldán said, "Why don't you boys ask Eduardo? He just returned from Haiti. They finished the documentary. He saw a voodoo woman in a trance bite the head off of a chicken."

Popeye and Luigi drove away to get the oil changed and to put air in the spare tire.

A few days later Popeye reappeared with Chuy, who had a bright red glove on his artificial hand.

Roldán was puzzled. "I thought you were going to Mexico City on Thursday."

Popeye dropped a quarter onto the window ledge to pay for a coffee. "There was an accident, gordo. Keep the change." He pointed to a shattered headlight. "It happened on the George Washington Bridge."

Chuy giggled. "We hit an enormous pigeon."

Popeye said, "There was nothing we could do. And anyway, the journey wouldn't have been much fun without Luigi."

"Where is Luigi?" I asked.

"He and his burnt face went to Montreal with a piba."

"What piba?"

"Adriana, Eduardo's ex-wife. Apparently they developed a friendship while Eduardo was in Haiti. Eduardo doesn't know yet."

Alfonso said, "When Eduardo finds out I bet the top of his head will blow off and sail up to the moon."

"But they're not even married," I pointed out.

Chuy scrutinized me as if I was a pitiable and deformed human being.

"Oh," he said, laying on the sarcasm. "I forgot. Then there's no problem."

49. You Scared Me!

After I bought a secondhand paperback at a bookstore on Fourth Avenue I walked up toward Fourteenth Street to gaze at some sexy posters in front of the burlesque theater. Next, I did a tour around Union Square. As I was back passing the outdoor bargain bins at S. Klein's I spotted Cathy Escudero ahead of me. Just as I realized it was her she filched a pretty red blouse, stuffing it quickly into her tote bag as she moved away. I ran a dozen steps and reached forward, touching her arm.

"Hola, Cathy."

She spun around with a look of frantic alarm, then realized it was me and her jaw dropped as she burst into tears.

"*Carajo, huevón, me espantaste, che!*"

"I didn't mean to scare you," I said. "Lo siento."

"Let's get out of here, blondie, quick." She grabbed my hand and tugged me around the corner onto University Place where we headed south toward NYU, almost running. It was all so sudden. Cathy searched right and left and repeatedly glanced backward to see if any cops were gaining on us. She wore a faded blue sweatshirt and old black slacks and sneakers, and her hair was in a ponytail. Without makeup her face was pale and blotchy.

She kept holding on to my hand as we hurried across to the west side of the street where she felt safer.

Cathy stopped abruptly in front of the Cedar Tavern and asked, "What were you doing, *following* me? Are you *crazy?*" Finally she let my hand go and rubbed the dampness from her cheeks and eye sockets. "I almost had a heart attack."

"I'm sorry," I said. "I'm really sorry. I wasn't following you. It was an accident. I didn't mean to scare you, I swear."

In Washington Square, Cathy sat us down on a bench near the children's play area. She reached into her tote bag, fumbling for lipstick and a compact, and went to work on her face. She brushed on powder, used a mascara pencil, and applied the lipstick, talking throughout the process.

"I don't have money so I steal," she explained. "I steal all my clothes. I steal everything. I steal food. I stole this lipstick, I stole these sneakers. I don't care. Everything I earn that doesn't go to my folks goes to my art. I pay my dance teacher. Jorge couldn't steal a pencil so I have to support him. He's helpless. You're almost like him except you have parents, and I bet they have money. If you're shy like Jorge you're dead in this world, blondie. The vultures will pick you to pieces in a minute. There. That's better."

She rubbed her lips together and observed her face at different angles in the compact mirror.

"*Damn,* you scared me," she said again.

"I'm so sorry," I said again.

"Quit saying you're sorry all the time. Girls hate that."

I shut up.

"I can't ever afford to get caught," Cathy said. She still looked like a frightened little girl. "If they catch you and you're a foreigner you're dead. They send you back to the trash bin. I hate this country because it's so vindictive."

I didn't know what to say.

Cathy looked at me.

"Are you still writing books?" she asked.

"Yes."

"I'm glad. Don't ever stop."

"I won't."

"Okay, let's go." Cathy kissed me lightly and stood up. "Enough hysterics. You can walk me to the subway."

She glanced around a final time to make sure no police agents were stalking us. There were kids in strollers, dogs on leashes, old men reading newspapers, couples on the grass, squirrels in the trees, but no cops.

Cathy held my hand all the way over to the Astor Place subway entrance where she patted my cheek, gave me a hug, then drew back and said, "You can't come to the dance studio anymore, blondie. Aurelio doesn't like it. No matter what I say he thinks you're a rival. *I'm* sorry."

She added scornfully, in English: "He doesn't know nothing about girls."

Then she said "I love you" in Spanish, squared her shoulders, and vanished underground.

Dumbfounded, I stared at the subway entrance.

When I got home there was a note with the travel agency logo on it stuck in my door. It said:

> I stopped by to say "hello." But
> you weren't here. Too bad, you
> lose. Call me at work sometime.
> Ciao,
> La Petisa

50. The Gift

I went to the hospital with Roldán when they were going to remove the cast from his arm. He needed an interpreter along to translate and help fill out the forms. At St. Vincent's an emergency room intern sawed off the cast and put it in a bag. He gave the fat man a tube of cream to rub onto his wrist and forearm. We stopped at the business office to settle up. A groggy bureaucrat asked me questions that I translated for Roldán who answered back and I told the bureaucrat, who wrote down the answers. A half hour later the paperwork was complete. Who knows how, but the cook escaped without paying a cent.

On the sidewalk we halted for a moment, blinking our eyes against the bright sun and the noisy bustle around us. My chubby friend bent his arm up and down, twisted his wrist, and flexed his fingers in and out. They were stiff, the muscles atrophied. His hand looked weird and tiny at the end of such a fat arm.

"Soon it'll be better than new," he said. "They did a good job. That's what I love about America."

We strolled at a leisurely pace to Sixth Avenue where the fat man paused at a flower vendor and purchased a dozen colorful carnations.

"Who are the flowers for?" I asked.

"For me, blondie. I deserve them."

We crossed the avenue and stopped at Johnny's Italian Newsstand for a cigar, then went down MacDougal to the empanada kiosk. It was shortly after one P.M.

"Come on up if you want," he said. "I've got a ham and some lemon meringue pie."

No thanks, I told him, I wanted to return to work. So I handed over the paper sack holding the two pieces of his cast. "Why don't you keep it?" Roldán said. "You're the writer. Perhaps you will make me famous one day."

I was surprised and deeply moved. "Really? You mean it?"

"Qué va." He gestured impatiently. "What do I want with stupid memorabilia?"

"Okay. Thanks a lot."

"A pleasure," he said. "I'm happy to be of service to you, Señor Hemingway."

Roldán shook my hand and went inside and climbed the stairs. It was painful to watch him through the glass door puffing at every step. If he met somebody they had to back up until he reached a landing where there was room to pass.

When I got home I laid both pieces of the cast on my kitchen table, poured a glass of milk, and contemplated the plaster of Paris creation. Everybody had signed it: Alfonso, Carlos the Artist and his wife, Gino, Eduardo, La Petisa, Chuy, Santiago Chávez, Greta Garbo, Luigi, and Popeye and even Eddie Ortega . . . but not Adriana, who had refused to sanctify anything contaminated by her ex-husband's John Hancock.

I spent ten minutes inspecting the cast, trying to decipher the salutations. La Petisa had drawn a funny little face with horns on top. Alfonso had written, *Sos un hombre, Patrón.* Eduardo had put, *Suerte, gordito!* Greta Garbo's said in English, *Good luck, baby!* Luigi and Popeye signed their names with a baroque flourish. And Carlos had taken up the most space with an elaborate sketch of a nude woman riding a large wingèd phallus. I couldn't read his handwriting.

Then I fitted the two halves together one atop the other and wrapped them carefully in newspaper, Scotch-taped the newspaper tightly shut, placed the bundle in a paper bag, and set the bag on the highest shelf of my kitchen cupboard for safekeeping.

51. Rock of Gibraltar

Cathy Escudero visited the empanada stand again, this time with Aurelio Porta. He had on a Panama hat, a tailored pin-striped suit, and tasseled loafers. She wore a blue velvet jersey, a black skirt, and high heels—very elegant. Her dark hair fell past her shoulders making her look truly sophisticated.

Alfonso, Carlos the Artist, and I hustled clear of the alley to let them in. Then we hung around on the sidewalk at the window. Everywhere pedestrians wearing short-sleeved shirts were talking and laughing.

Roldán said, "Hello, beautiful. Whatever you want, I invite you. It's on the house."

Cathy smiled, delighted. Men were always giving her stuff for nothing. She leaned over the counter and kissed the patrón, leaving a red imprint on his sweaty cheek. She ordered a beef empanada, a dulce de leche, and a Coke. Aurelio Porta asked for black coffee and a quince pie. Roldán clicked on his fan to blow away some of the smoke.

"I'm so happy," Cathy announced. "Aurelio and I are engaged. We're going to be married this June in Uruguay. The wedding will be at a big country club where Aurelio plays polo. A week later I'm going to open at La Taberna Gitana in Buenos Aires. We'll visit Patagonia on our honeymoon. Look at my diamond ring. Isn't it beautiful?"

She held it up, her fingers spread wide for effect.

Alfonso said, "It's bigger than the Rock of Gibraltar."

Carlos asked, "How much did a boulder like that set you back?"

Cathy kissed the diamond affectionately. "Two hundred and seventy-three dollars. It's from Tiffany's. Aurelio gave it to me yesterday. To celebrate, we had dinner at the Stork Club. I'm so in love with him I could dance right out of my skin." She kissed Aurelio's earlobe and tweaked his chin and ran her hand through his long curly hair.

Aurelio smiled.

"My novio has a ten-room house in Montevideo," Cathy continued. "And a black Citroën automobile. He's going to teach me how to drive the car and ride horses and shoot live pigeons at the country club."

Roldán passed over the empanadas, the coffee, the Coke, and the dulce de leche. He also picked up a stack of paper cups and handed one to Aurelio, one to Cathy, and one to each of the rest of us. From under the grease bin he fetched a half-empty bottle of red wine, pried the cork out with his teeth, and poured each of us a splash. Then he raised his cup, saying, "Here's to the boda."

Everyone repeated in unison, "Health, love, money . . . and all the time in the world to spend them!"

"I am going to be married in a dress of red velvet," Cathy said. "I will carry two dozen white roses for my bouquet. My flower girls will wear white satin with elbow-length gloves and beautiful opaque stockings. There will be an orchestra and the best flamenco guitarist in Montevideo—Enrique Barrón. I will dance alegrías at my own reception. The champagne will come from France."

We all stared at the dancer, hanging on to every word. She was shining like an autumn maple leaf made even more radiant by rain. If huge ruby ribbons carried by naked cherubs with pink wings had appeared over her head nobody would have been surprised.

After Cathy and Aurelio Porta left the kiosk we moved back inside the cozy cubicle. Roldán emptied the dregs of his wine bottle into our cups. We tingled from being seduced by Cathy's youthful enthusiasm.

Alfonso lifted his cup. "Here's to the lucky couple. They certainly deserve each other."

We drank to that.

52. Counting Sheep

I was stunned by Cathy's news.

Even when you see it coming for months it catches you by surprise.

I walked home to Prince and West Broadway and climbed the stairs toward my apartment. There was an odor of garlic and cooking oil on the second landing. Higher, through a door opened a crack, I heard people talking about food in English with Italian accents. But I didn't feel hungry.

Sitting in the dark at my own apartment window I gazed down at Prince Street. It was quiet, the storefronts dark, the garbage cans lined up for collection tomorrow. Faint jukebox music came from Milady's Bar on the Thompson Street corner, and the warm bread smell arose from Vesuvio's bakery. Beyond the black silhouettes of water towers atop neighborhood tenements the night sky glowed a misty pink. Midtown skyscrapers seemed very distant. The blinking lights of an airplane were headed toward La Guardia.

I could not relax and stayed up for hours, fidgeting, pacing between my kitchen and the bedroom. I wanted to kill myself, but how? I leafed through books by a handful of famous writers, reading a few paragraphs or a few pages, unable to concentrate. For a while I tried to type, a mistake; I gave up impatiently. I almost kicked apart the manuscripts piled neatly across my floor, but didn't. I tore all the rejection slips and postcards off my bulletin board, crumpled them up, and fired them one by one into the wastebasket. I even took a bath but couldn't sit still long enough to enjoy it. So I made a cheese sandwich and drank three cups of instant coffee as I contemplated Prince Street again. Nothing happened, though, not even a taxi drifted by.

Then I looked for the note La Petisa had left in my door but I couldn't find it. It was not in my wallet, nor tacked to the bulletin board, nor on my typing table or a windowsill, nor atop any of my manuscripts, nor in any pocket of my shirts and pants or my jacket. Shit. It was just gone, period.

Okay. I put on my jacket and knitted cap and went downstairs to the sidewalk. I prowled north on West Broadway which was deserted. I felt miserable, like a fool, a patsy, a clown. I wanted to walk over to the East River and jump off a bridge. *So long, blondie.* Splash! Me and Virginia Woolf. All the metal city trash baskets were filled to overflowing. In a doorway between Houston and Bleecker a bum was conked out, one leg bent underneath himself at an awkward angle. The Grand Union in front of the NYU projects was dark. A man and a woman holding hands walked by me headed south. "I didn't like it," she said. "You weren't paying attention," he replied.

A cop car idled beneath the Washington Square arch, its headlights turned off. A guy was walking a large dog on the diagonal through the park. I circled the empty fountain afraid of those officers who might be watching me, invisible inside their dark cruiser.

If they'd known what I was thinking they would have jumped out and tackled me, clapped on the cuffs, thrown me into a dungeon, and left me there to rot.

I traveled south on Thompson Street because I didn't want to pass all the shuttered-up seedy clip joints on MacDougal or see the empanada stand. The deserted area during the wee hours looked shabby and cheap. It sure fit my mood. I heard a cop's horse clip-clopping west of me. A taxi with its OFF DUTY sign illuminated went slowly past. Steam leaked up from a Con Ed grate. Concrete slabs were broken at a construction site circled by yellow warning tape. I almost stepped on a dog turd.

Fuck this city.

I climbed back to my apartment and sat in the dark some more looking out the window. No lights were lit in the buildings across from me so I could not even be a voyeur. I couldn't be anything. My writing stunk. I had no money. I was still a virgin. *Life is a tale told by an idiot, full of sound and fury, signifying nothing.*

After a spell of thinking like that I lay on my bed and stared at the ceiling, literally counting sheep. Just for spite I counted over three thousand, which wasn't easy. There's no logical or acceptable way to deal with heartbreak. Then I fell asleep.

53. Insults

When Eduardo learned that Luigi had "eloped" with Adriana he went crazy. Arriving at the empanada stand black with rage he rambled on about betrayal. He accused Roldán, Alfonso, Carlos the Artist, and even me of aiding and abetting the romance. "I want to garotte all of you cowards with my bare hands." He called us fairies, said Roldán was a "fat old pederast" and Alfonso was "a diminutive queer." For good measure he called Carlos a "lascivious sodomizer." Though he tried to pick a fight with everyone nobody gave him the satisfaction. Finally he broke down, tearfully accusing America of destroying his life. "All us muchachos were insane to leave Argentina."

It made him delirious to think of Adriana captured by the arms of that ugly dwarf. What an insult to his manhood, to her womanhood, and to male/female relationships in general. Had she no shame at all?

"Dale, che, at least he's a fellow Argentine," Roldán noted.

Eduardo laughed like a condemned man on the gallows. "Yeah. Thank God for small favors," he sneered.

Right then Eddie Ortega popped up at the window in an aggressive mood. When the boss gave the little ferret some money, Eddie counted it and proceeded to break the rules, barking aloud for everyone to hear: "That's not enough, panzón. What do I look like, a dope?"

Eduardo instantly broke the rules in retaliation: "Hey, get out of here you piece of garbage. Go fuck yourself!"

Eddie Ortega looked surprised. Then he fled, terrified, as Eduardo took a wild swing and also tried to kick him.

54. A Ticket Out of the Ghetto

Alfonso met me in front of the Bleecker Street Cinema. We were going to see a movie by Jean-Luc Godard. As we stood in line for the tickets, Alfonso said, "Did you hear what happened to Jorge?"

"The guitarist for Cathy Escudero?"

"Yes, that guy—the young boy."

"No, what happened?"

"He killed himself. Chuy told me."

I accepted my ticket and the change from the ticket seller. I couldn't believe it. Alfonso bought his ticket and we went inside. The theater was crowded but we found seats in the middle of a row toward the back. Alfonso *ahh*ed against his glasses and wiped them clean on his scarf.

"How did he kill himself?" I asked.

"Out the window of his apartment into the air shaft. Six stories up. He smashed all the garbage cans."

"How could he do that?"

"I guess it was a broken heart. People die for that reason all the time."

"He wasn't even eighteen." My ears had started ringing.

"Adolescence is the most vulnerable time."

Alfonso removed a small box of raisins from his pocket and offered me some. Underneath the purple scarf he wore a baggy gray sweater knitted by Sofía.

"He was a great guitar player," I said. "I mean . . ." I was at a loss for words. I felt dizzy, cold, flushed.

Alfonso said, "Well, he's playing his guitar in heaven now while that arrogant dancer prepares to drink French champagne."

"Where is his family?" I asked.

"In Sevilla. A brother named Eliverio flew over and took back the body and his guitars. Jorge had four guitars and lived in a one-room crib with a mattress on the floor. The maestro Alejandro Cárdenas says he might have been good one day."

"I can't even remember why he was in the United States."

"Cárdenas was his teacher over there. They say the old maestro committed a political crime and fled to New York where he has a cousin. In Spain, if you spit on the street Franco's goons will kill you just as quickly as they shot García Lorca. So Jorge flew to America to be with his teacher. Cathy Escudero paid him to play for her. As you know, she earned her money working at El Parrillón on Forty-seventh Street. She also studies once a week with Matilde Guerrero. Both those kids believed that flamenco was a ticket out of the ghetto."

"I can't believe he would do a thing like that," I said. I couldn't think straight. My stomach was cramping. I had trouble breathing correctly.

Alfonso finished off the raisins. "When you're really in love you're helpless," he explained. "When you are obsessed—when your heart is hog-tied by a woman—you go crazy. It's a dangerous situation. You know that my Renata is like that. She laughs and is full of fire and has terrible moods and drinks too much. She is either too happy or too sad or too angry. She writes poetry and knows how to ice-skate. Her beautiful long hair makes my chest ache. With her I am a yo-yo, up and down, perpetually off balance and confused. Of course I would die for her and I would kill for her, too. After a while this condition can be fatal. I just want to escape."

"But you love her?"

"Love." He sighed. "Who knows about that? Cervantes said war and love are the same thing."

"Hey, shuttup," said a guy behind us. "We're trying to watch the movie."

Alfonso turned around, speaking English. "*You* shut up, buddy. A man just died for love and we're talking about him."

Another moviegoer said, "Pipe down you assholes."

"Fuck you," Alfonso said. "And your mother and your little sister, too."

"Take off your glasses," said the first person, "and I'll teach you to be rude."

Alfonso stood up. "Come on, blondie, let's get out of here."

People booed and hissed as we squeezed clear of the row. One fellow slapped at my leg. Out on the sidewalk Alfonso removed his glasses and wiped his eyes and cheeks on his scarf. We walked up to Washington Square where some old men were playing chess under the streetlamps. After kibitzing for a minute we headed diagonally through the park to the corner of University Place. Turning left, we traveled west to MacDougal Street, then south to the bottom of the square, then east again. I kept visualizing Jorge falling among the garbage cans but I couldn't say a word. Feelings of guilt and confusion made me tongue-tied. My heart was beating too fast. I wondered who had told Cathy Escudero, and what had her reaction been? Alfonso was quiet also, lost in his own thoughts. We made the rounds five times in this manner before splitting up and heading off toward our separate apartments.

Alfonso stopped and turned around, calling after me, "Are you okay?"

I was not, but you know how it is with guys: I said, "Yes."

55. Guitar Lessons

I entered a pawnshop on Second Avenue and East Third Street and asked the big lug behind the grill how much for a Stella guitar in his window? He said, "Ten bucks." I handed over the money, so he came forward and leaned into the window fetching the guitar.

"This is a lousy instrument," he admitted. "Are you sure you want it?"

"It's the only one I can afford."

I don't know why, but he pointed out, "The neck is warped. If you don't have calluses it'll destroy your fingers."

I didn't care. I took the guitar and walked west on Houston Street, then up to the empanada stand. Alfonso was alone in the alley talking to Roldán about the mysterious stone heads on Easter Island. I gave the Stella to Alfonso, asking would he please tune it for me? Even though he could not play, the professor knew how to tune a guitar. He started right in and immediately scowled.

"This is a bad instrument, blondie."

"I don't care. Just tune it, please."

"Maybe I can't. The neck is terrible. The strings are so old they're rusted."

"I spent all my money. That's it. Do the best you can."

He did as well as could be expected. Then I went home and opened my new Mel Bay *Chords for Beginners* book and started teaching myself C, F, and G7.

It was nearly impossible to press down the metal strings, let alone strike a note that sounded halfway decent. Nevertheless, I spent all afternoon learning those three chords. I stroked them slowly with my thumb or flopped my fingers back and forth in a sloppy rhythm. I tried some clumsy arpeggios. Could I will myself instantly to be a musician? By the end of the afternoon my fingers were sore and I had grown depressed. But I kept on until dark.

Then I sat at my tin table and rolled a fresh piece of paper into the typewriter. I proceeded to write a three-page short story that was so cloying I shredded it immediately into a hundred pieces.

The next day I learned E, A, and B7. Also A, D, and E7. My left fingertips ached and my right thumb had a blister. Finally I gave up and sat quietly for an hour holding the guitar on my lap while staring out the window. A man on a roof across the street was cleaning a pigeon cage as his birds circled the neighborhood. I could see the Empire State Building far north on Thirty-third Street.

Around four P.M. I left the apartment carrying my guitar and headed up West Broadway to Washington Square. It was a lazy warm day; cherry trees at the kids' play area had blossomed. People were throwing Frisbees near a volleyball game behind the fountain. Some guys from the Caribbean thumped loudly on conga drums.

I sat on a bench observing the scene. Finally a beatnik sauntered over. "Hey, man, can I take a look at your ax?"

I handed him the instrument as he sat down beside me. Laboriously, his fingers made a C chord. When he plucked it the sound was terrible. "Wow, that's cool," he said.

"It's all yours." I stood up. "Te lo regalo."

He gawked at me but I walked away, going south to the empanada stand to see what was happening. Roldán had the window open but the place was still closed as he heated up the grease bin and prepared for the evening commerce. The sidewalks were crowded with tourists.

"What's new in Kalamazoo?" the cook asked me in English, and laughed. That was another expression I had taught him.

I said, "Nada, nada, nada, nada."

"Where's that spiffy guitar?" he asked in Spanish. "Are you ready to put Segovia out of business?"

"I gave it to a guy in the park."

Roldán said, "Oh." But he was a discreet man and never asked me why I had bought it nor why I gave it away.

56. Grief

I rode the subway uptown and walked east to El Parrillón. You had to step down in the stairwell and pull open the door. Just inside there was an old-fashioned coatrack. A few tables were occupied and a half dozen guys wearing business suits sat at the bar smoking cigarettes. There were dominoes on the bar and a leather dice cup. Subdued Latin music played in the background.

Two waitresses were handling the tables and one was Cathy Escudero. At the center of each table was a thin glass vase with a carnation in it and beside the vase stood three small bottles of condiments. A smoky odor defined the area; it came from meat being grilled in the open kitchen on the east side of the room.

Cathy looked up the second I entered and didn't even blink. A man at the hostess station handed me a menu, but Cathy had come right over, lifted it from his hand, put it down, and led me to one side. She was holding a glass pitcher of ice water. Her hair was pulled back in a bun held tightly by invisible netting. She had mascara around her eyes but no lipstick. Her eyes seemed too large and they were bloodshot. The skin above her cheekbones was bruised from fatigue. She wore a pastel rose-colored blouse and pleated blue trousers and soft brown shoes. Not a hint of flamboyance colored the outfit.

"Blondie," she said, "what are you doing up here?"

"I heard about Jorge. I'm really sorry. I don't know what to do. I don't know what to say."

She said, "You can't do anything about dead people. Son difuntos. When they die it's over. You're stuck with the memories."

"I know, but . . ."

"It's not my fault. I didn't kill him. We weren't lovers. I never touched him privately."

I shook my head. "No, I understand . . . I didn't mean . . . it's not . . ."

"I will find another guitarist. Because I'm an artist I can deal with tragedy. This won't stop me. What do you think all art is about? If Jorge chose to kill himself, I respect him for that. And don't you dare intrude on my feelings. I come from a world you can't imagine."

Perhaps I moved my hands in a gesture of condolence, I don't know, but I was stymied.

Cathy said, "Weak people are always the ones you cherish most. But if you let them control your life you're fucked. I'm not ready to die yet and you aren't either. Now, I'm at work here, I have to earn a living. Go mourn for Jorge like a man."

I asked, "Are you still getting married?"

"Yes I am. But I have to earn money for my parents before we leave because Aurelio won't give them a penny."

I summoned all my courage to speak, but she put her fingertips against my lips. Cathy's eyes glistened from tears that she was refusing to let fall. "Don't say it, blondie. You'll embarrass both of us. Grow up and leave me alone with my grief."

I hesitated.

She said in English, "*Please.*"

Then she turned away from me and went back to waiting tables. She poured water from her pitcher without splashing out the ice. She opened a bottle of wine and filled three glasses. Moving gracefully, she attended to her tables without a hint of subservience. I watched her for a moment longer and then I pushed open the door, climbed to the sidewalk, and went home.

57. Flying to Morocco

Ten days later Alfonso asked me, "Why weren't you at Carlos's art show the other night, blondie? We missed you. It was a great success."

"I was sulking. I'm tired of listening to Spanish all the time. And I got my old job back at the Night Owl when they reopened. It keeps me busy."

The truth is I had been shell-shocked and in mourning with no one to talk to. In mourning for Jorge, and also for Cathy Escudero. And for the dream I'd had in college of being an artist in New York. Tragedy was not romantic, it was awful. I felt like a confused animal stranded on a rooftop in a flood.

"Yes, the show received some good reviews," Roldán said. "Although Carlos himself was drunk and had to be carried to a taxi. Nevertheless, it was a triumph. The gallery has already sold three paintings."

Alfonso showed us a postcard he had received from Luigi, postmarked Montreal.

The message said:

> Bonjour, mecs,
> Having a great time here.
> How were the bullfights in Mexico
> City?
> À bientôt,
> Luigi

"What about Gino?" I asked. "Has he been around lately?"

Alfonso said Gino was working on Fifth Avenue and Fifty-third Street in a clothing store. "He's earning a lot of money and has moved uptown. I think he is becoming Cosa Nostra. He runs with a pretty tough group and uses greasy hair lotion."

I stated the obvious: "Apparently I'm not the only one who hasn't been showing up at the kiosk."

"It's spring," Roldán said. "There are no cold winds to drive them here. I myself might visit Spain. I've approached several banks for a loan."

Come again? Jesus, *that* startled me. "What would you do in Spain?"

"Oh, travel a bit. Scramble for a peseta. I'll hit Madrid first to see friends. Then maybe head north to Santander or San Sebastián. I'll open a food emporium near the sea, buy a bathing suit. I'm looking for a place to settle down and that could be just the ticket. San Sebastián especially. On Sundays after the bullfights life will be relaxed. Good cognac with Basques and Gallegos. I expect to have a ball."

Before I could comment, Eduardo popped his head through the window. "Congratulate me," he ordered us. "I have a new wife and a new job with CBS and I am bankrupt. But now I could become a director of New Wave films."

"You married again after the last lesson?" Alfonso was amazed.

Eduardo said, "It couldn't be helped. I dreamed about her and when I woke up there she was. A miracle. Her name is Molly, she's American. We got hitched that same day. A very good-looking kid who's an intern on a CBS camera crew." He handed out a cheap cigar to each of us. "Adriana? Who is

Adriana? I forgot her already. She and Luigi have evaporated like smoke."

"That's what happened to my nylons business," Popeye said as he arrived at the window with a patch over one eye. "Give me a mate, patrón."

Then he recounted his recent change in fortune: "I'm now employed at a supermarket dusting soup cans and tomatoes. I like the job. I have a big feather brush and wear an apron. They give me the bruised tomatoes for free. I rearrange potatoes and stack cucumbers and spray mist on the lettuce. I also polish apples and throw away rotten bananas. If a shopper drops a mayonnaise jar I run to clean up the mess. My rent is overdue, I can't pay the electric bill, the cockroaches are even in my refrigerator, and I haven't been laid for a week. But last night on the subway I met a sexy Asian babe who gave me her telephone number."

La Petisa next appeared from the wings and took over center stage.

She said, "You never give up, do you, marinero? I would think it'd be worn out by now. What happened to your eye?"

"I bumped into a fist," Popeye said, but he refused to elaborate. He accepted a cigar from Eduardo, though, and La Petisa did also.

Then she held up one hand for attention and dropped her little bomb on us. "I came here to say good-bye, boys. On Saturday I'm flying to Morocco. I've had it with the United States. I plan to learn Arabic. Don't you think that will be fun?"

"*Morocco?*" I blurted, astonished. "For God's sake, what will you do in Morocco?"

She grinned and tweaked my chin. "Wouldn't you like to know, blondie? But you're too late. I gave you a chance and you didn't take it. I'll send you a postcard from Casablanca, however. I already have your address in my book."

Roldán said, "Change your plans, nena. Sail with me to Spain. We could have a good time. I'll pay for your ticket."

"You're a sweetie, gordo." She rose on tiptoes and leaned over the windowsill to kiss his cheek. "But no thanks. I have other fish to fry."

The cook laughed, cocking his head, spreading wide his arms. "Why do all the girls avoid me? In his lifetime every man should plant a tree, write a book, and have a child. I'm forty-seven years old already, but I have done none of those things."

"You have a lot of time left," I said.

"What do you know about time, blondie?"

Alfonso said, "Quit picking on him. When the right day comes you will plant a tree. *And* write a book."

"Maybe in Spain," the fat man said. "I apologize, blondie. I'm just kidding around."

They all seemed happy and everyone except me lit a cigar, sending forth great puffs of smoke to honor Eduardo and Molly's nuptials and La Petisa's upcoming voyage. After that, La Petisa kissed Alfonso good-bye, she kissed Popeye, Roldán, and Eduardo also. When it came my turn she gave me an extra-big hug and planted a wet one squarely on my mouth, causing the boys to clap enthusiastically, and Alfonso even whistled.

Then she ruffled her hand in my hair and waved at the guys, and ran away before we could tell if she was crying.

58. ¡Qué Quilombo!

Luigi and Adriana returned to New York after their adventures in Montreal. "We made love five times a day," Luigi bragged to us at the kiosk. "She couldn't keep her hands off me. Me devoraba con una rapacidad vertiginosa."

He checked his watch. "Oops, it's late, I'll bet she's waiting for me in a black negligee." He paid his tab and hurried off.

The next morning Adriana showed up at CBS and physically assaulted Eduardo's new wife. She grabbed Molly's hair, kicked her in the groin, and yanked her cashmere sweater off. A dozen male technicians had to restrain her. They hustled Adriana to Eduardo's office where the young producer bawled her out but declined to call the gendarmes.

Molly wanted to press charges but Eduardo said no. So Molly and Eduardo had a blistering fight. Simultaneously, Luigi threw a temper tantrum, accusing Adriana of being an unfaithful prostitute. The volatile lady immediately packed her bags and fled. Luigi then barged in on Eduardo at CBS demanding to know where Adriana was hiding. They got into a shouting match and security guards railroaded Luigi out the emergency exit.

Tearfully, Molly accused Eduardo of cheating on her with his ex-wife. Eduardo denied it but he was lying. Luigi got drunk and threatened to disembowel both Eduardo and Adriana. When Molly left Eduardo and filed for divorce, Adriana promptly reappeared, cozy as a bunny in Eduardo's apartment. Luigi went to CBS again, but now he shook Eduardo's hand, saying, "The best guy won," and he ducked out of the office a free man, leaving Eduardo puzzled and slightly irritated, wondering: Am I the winner or the loser in this mess?

At the empanada stand Luigi said, "I just spent weeks spinning in a cyclone. What a relief that it's over."

He spoke too soon. Molly made a terrible scene at Eduardo's office and was fired by CBS. She came to the kiosk looking for Luigi, who tried to hide by squatting down in the alley behind me and Alfonso. But his coffee cup and half-eaten pastelito on the counter ledge gave him away.

"He's crouching down there like a scared little frog, isn't he?" Molly was blonde, blue-eyed, healthy, and wholesome—an alien creature unable to speak a word of Spanish.

Luigi straightened up, asking Alfonso to translate. Alfonso said to Molly, "What do you want?"

"I want you to help me nail Eduardo to the cross."

"Why?"

"What do you mean, *why*?" Molly was flabbergasted that the burnt man would hesitate even one second to begin plotting revenge.

But Luigi was no dope. "I have nothing against Eduardo," he said nervously. "He's my pal."

Molly sized him up for five seconds. Then she asked, "Doesn't it rankle that Adriana dropped you like a bad habit and started fucking Eduardo again?"

We were shocked by the obscenity issuing from such a well-bred lady's mouth.

Alfonso, translating for Luigi, said, "What do you see in Eduardo? He's a two-bit hack, a petty thief, a vapid egomaniac." In Spanish Luigi had not said "vapid egomaniac," but rather "conchudo," which means "filthy cunt."

Molly said, "I love him, I'm sorry."

The professor could not resist. "*Love?*" he teased her, and then quoted Cervantes in full: "'Love and War are the same thing, and stratagems and policy are as allowable in the one as in the other.'"

Molly gave him the finger.

59. Balmy Weather

"It's a fact the patrón is heading for Spain," Alfonso said. "He wasn't just kidding around. He told me yesterday that he bought a ticket a month ago. The boat leaves in five days."

A month ago? What next? We were strolling across Washington Square enjoying toasted almond Good Humors and the balmy weather. Gorgeous women were everywhere. A jug band was playing by the fountain.

When I asked Alfonso *why* the cook was leaving, he gave me the bad news: "He screwed up, he's in hock too deep. The loan sharks are pissed off. Some checks bounced at the bank. He even has gambling debts and hasn't paid the rent for two months. Roldán is a terrible businessman. He'll wind up incarcerated or at the bottom of the East River if he doesn't get out of here soon."

"That's terrible," I said.

Alfonso gestured almost cavalierly. "It's not too bad, blondie. He's been there before. It's his modus operandi. Yet he always escapes."

"But what will we do when he leaves?" I asked. "All the guys in our patota. The kiosk is where we meet."

Alfonso sat down on a bench and I took my place beside him. A curly-haired tot sped by us furiously pedaling her tricycle. Suddenly I knew that more sad facts were about to be revealed.

The professor said, "Look, I've been meaning to tell you, blondie. I'm going home to Buenos Aires soon. I really miss my country. I'll finish my doctorate there. I plan to marry Sofía, the boring old friend, and stop talking to idiots before I become one myself."

Removing his glasses he wiped them clean on his shirttail while I frowned and studied my fingernails.

"Of course *you* are not an idiot," Alfonso added. "But you know what I mean. Gino and Popeye and Chuy are not exactly Einsteins."

When I could speak I said, "Sofía will be good for you. She'll be an anchor in the storm."

"Yes, Sofía is wonderful. She's intelligent and polite and extremely loyal. I could cheat on her with a dozen Renatas and she'd still love me. Renata would castrate me if she learned I was unfaithful."

"Is that your plan, to marry Sofía so you can cheat on her with a hundred Renatas?"

"Don't be a dumbbell, che." Alfonso was embarrassed and a little angry. He flicked his wooden ice-cream stick toward a nearby trash basket. "Melodrama aside, blondie, the truth is I am a funny little man with glasses who hasn't been laid in a year and I'm so horny I could die. Too bad, tough luck. Yes, Renata is the one big adventure of my life, but I'm also a mathematical genius. And this way, if I marry the calm pragmatic Sofía instead of the wild and crazy Renata, I can do a lot for math. Also, we'll have a family and, as I've said before, I will learn to love her."

"You don't sound very happy about your decision, profe."

"Of course I'm not happy. I'm human, aren't I? I adore Renata. I *lust* for Renata. I jerk off every night *thinking* about Renata."

He paused, wondering if he should have admitted that. Then he said quietly, with intense feeling, "But I also want to survive."

I considered this statement for a moment. Then I said, "Let's do something to give Roldán a royal send-off. He's probably broke because of us. It doesn't seem we ever gave much to him. Why not a big going-away party? We'll gather everybody and take him to Chinatown for dinner. He loves sweet-and-sour pork—"

"Stop." Alfonso shook his head. "We can't tell anybody else that he's leaving. Roldán is skipping out on the gangsters, and if they learn about it beforehand who knows what might happen?"

We sat there a few moments longer touched by the afternoon shadows. It seemed impossible to me how things that were so precious could be dismantled so quickly. Squirrels were having a field day in the branches overhead and pigeons swooped against the blue sky. Members of the jug band were on a cigarette break.

At length Alfonso said, "Don't be sad. Things always change. The patota is just a figment of our imaginations."

Then he added, "One day I'll come back with my wife and kids to visit you, blondie, wherever you are. Perhaps we'll be grown-ups by then."

60. Face-to-Face

The night before he headed to Spain, Roldán closed the empanada stand early. A few of us in on the secret stayed behind to dismantle the operation before his landlord or a loan shark could tip that the cook was taking a powder. Popeye double-parked the diaper truck nearby and brought over some cardboard boxes. Chuy paid off a cop to ignore our vehicle. Alfonso and I carried cartons of stuff to the truck. Leftover empanadas and pastelitos, salt shakers, Tabasco bottles, coffee cans and packs of napkins, dish soap, bags of yerba mate, a crate of Cokes, and so forth. We lugged over the coffee machine. There were little saucers and a few mate drinking straws, called bombillas, and various cooking utensils.

The boss had made a deal with Chuy for the entire lot. Chuy had a Mexican pal from Guanajuato who was setting up a café in Brooklyn. So he purchased Roldán's meager inventory for a hundred dollars and change.

We cleaned out the kiosk in half an hour like piranhas attacking an unfortunate tapir that had fallen into their river.

Next, we raced upstairs and did the same thing to his apartment. Popeye had string for bundling the old newspapers before we carted them down to the garbage cans. Luigi and Alfonso packed up Roldán's books, which were destined for Santiago Chávez, his baker. I emptied the refrigerator of what little remained, fodder for my larder.

On the spot Chuy bought the TV set for twenty dollars, then gave it to Luigi.

The naked Christmas tree had a couple of bulbs still blinking so we didn't touch it. Three large flimsy suitcases reinforced by knotted twine stood ready near the door. After we had swept clean the floors and washed the final dishes, Popeye and Luigi went to move the diaper truck since the cop was getting nervous. Chuy tagged after them because he had a date with his accountant, Greta Garbo.

And Alfonso took off, dog tired, leaving me alone with the cocinero.

There would be no brass bands or birthday hats; no last commemoration by his friends. Roldán was leaving New York by the back door, just one step ahead of the mob. The collapse had come about so quickly. I wanted to apologize but resisted the temptation. How could I deal with all that had occurred of late?

We sat at the kitchen table sharing a last two copas of wine. For all his heft the cook seemed fragile and tired. He had on a white guayabera shirt, baggy blue trousers, and sandals. His watch had a corroded golden stretch band. As always, his cheeks and his neck glistened from sweat and he wheezed while breathing. We clinked rims—"Salud!"—and began drinking the wine.

The fat man said, "Well, blondie, this is the end of the road in America. Thank you for helping me out tonight."

"I'm going to miss you, Roldán."

Embarrassed, he brushed that aside with his hand. "No importa. You're young," he said. "Your whole life is in front of you. You will be married, you'll have kids, you'll own a car someday, I bet. Maybe you'll even be rich."

"I'm going to miss you, Roldán," I said again, taking a sip of wine.

My corpulent friend poured himself a refill and flicked imaginary crumbs off his shirt.

"I think you will be a good writer one day," he said. "I've been watching you. You listen to everything that people say and you never interrupt. You know all our secrets, but refuse to reveal any of your own."

The cook dipped a finger in his glass; he licked it. He thought for a moment. Then he reached across the table and clasped my hand. "Listen. No matter how hard you try you can't make people love you in spite of themselves. And you can't stop them from committing suicide, either. That's just the way it is."

"I'm really going to miss you," I said once more.

The life drained from his features leaving him ashen, obviously exhausted.

"I'm tired, blondie. Go home to sleep." And in English he said, "Don't let the bedbugs bite."

That, too, I had taught him.

61. Adiós, Cocinero

Come morning, Alfonso, Luigi, and I took Roldán in a taxi over to the pier. For me it was very painful. At the boat we carried the fat man's suitcases to his cabin and then located a ballroom bar and drank a bottle of champagne. Alfonso gave the cook a box with two going-away presents: a cap pistol and a battered canteen. Both these objects he had found on the street recently.

"The canteen is so that you will not thirst on the road ahead," he explained. "And the pistol is to take care of your enemies, if ever you have any, which I sincerely doubt."

Each of us gave him a large and long abrazo. Many "good-byes" were said, and numerous "go with Gods." Luigi and Alfonso linked arms to serenade Roldán with "Adiós, Muchachos," the most famous tango ever sung by Carlos Gardel:

So long, boys, I'm off, I'm all
worn out, I'm sorry,
But against my fate there is no
point in crying;
Those great parties for me now
they are all over,
Because my body is so tired and
I am dying.

After leaving Roldán we waited around on the pier until the embarkation. We waved, and were showered by streamers and confetti as the ship pulled away heading for Spain. We kept blowing kisses.

"He will never plant that tree," Alfonso remarked sadly. "Or write a book."

I asked, "Why do you say that?"

"It's the way he is. It's in his genes."

We stopped at a bucket of blood on Eleventh Avenue for a final shot to the maestro's bon voyage. Afterward, we rode the subway downtown, getting off at Sheridan Square. And then something happened: All three of us felt bereft. We wanted to stick together a while longer and so we started walking.

Of course, when you are young and healthy and poor in New York City you do a lot of walking. Much of it is aimless, and all the while you are looking at people and thinking about things, excited to be alive even when you are miserable. Or occasionally you are so muddled by despair that everything passes before your eyes dispassionately and you don't care about anything or anybody.

The day that Roldán sailed for Spain I walked all over Manhattan with Alfonso and Luigi. It was a marathon. We left Greenwich Village, traveling down through the Financial District to Battery Park, then turned around and went all the way uptown to Columbus Circle. We crossed Central Park to the Metropolitan but did not enter the museum. We headed south after that on Fifth Avenue to Washington Square Park, then east across the alphabet avenues and through the Jacob Riis projects to the river. From there we descended to the Manhattan Bridge, bore west on Canal to West Broadway, and hiked back up to Washington Square. We began at noon on a Monday and finished up at six the next morning.

What did we talk about? Life and death and centuries of history and the politics of the United States and Latin America and the Soviet Union. We discussed existentialism and the transcendentalists and the atomic bomb and love. We analyzed movies: *Il Bell'Antonio, The Seventh Seal, Rocco and His Brothers.* Alfonso went on at great length about his Argentine lovers—Renata, the unstable psychotic paramour, and Sofía, the steadfast practical pal. Luigi regaled us with tales of Montreal and Adriana. But I shied away from Cathy Escudero. We had a heated give-and-take about artists who self-destruct, like Dylan Thomas and Baudelaire. Alfonso sang a few tangos and a couple of songs by Violeta Parra of Chile. Luigi performed an aria from *Rigoletto.* I sang tunes by Elvis Presley and Chuck Berry and Little Richard.

When we stopped to eat—at an Automat, a Greek gyro joint, a delicatessen—we never tarried for long indoors. We wanted to stay in motion.

When we began our journey we did not know it would last so long or cover that much ground. None of us wanted to stop and look at things, we were too engrossed in our conversation. I do not remember many of the particulars, only that we never quit speaking to one another. At the end we were exhausted. When it came time to split up, go home, and sleep, Alfonso framed my face between his hands and kissed me on the lips with fervor, man to man.

He said, "I am sorry for all the sorrows on this planet, blondie. Thank God we can still rejoice."

Then we three tottered off to our little apartments.

And a week later the professor caught a plane to Argentina where he married practical Sofía, whom he did not love, instead of the glamorous and unstable Renata, whom he adored.

62. Last Words and Despedidas

Áureo Roldán had pulled the plug on our patota when he closed the empanada stand and went to Spain. Abruptly we were all scattered about the city with no place to meet. Around the middle of June, however, I ran into Popeye and Luigi at the Eighth Avenue subway's Spring Street station. I greeted them like water at a desert oasis. They had old suitcases in hand and were heading for the Port Authority where they planned to catch a bus to Acapulco. Their papers were in order, yet the U.S. Army had been nosing around and they did not want to be drafted. I rode with them to the Port Authority, but there was a last-minute rush so we had no time for a farewell copa. Just before he stepped onto the bus, though, Luigi gripped both my shoulders and said, "You're going to be a star, blondie. I bet you publish a book next year. And then they will make it into a popular movie, okay?"

"Okay."

I did not tell them that my college romance had now been rejected six times.

"In Acapulco we're going to start a restaurant," Popeye called out a window as the Greyhound left its dock, "and in one year we'll return to New York as millionaires!"

After that I saw nobody until I bumped into Eduardo on the boardwalk at Coney Island in July. He was with a new woman, not Molly nor Adriana, and had grown a full beard. Soon after the divorce from Molly all excitement from the affair with his first wife had vanished. "I have been to Las Vegas making movies," he said. "Next week I'm flying to Los Angeles. I think I will stay there for good. I am twice an adulterer in New York state now, and after three times don't they make you stay married for good?"

He then pulled a surprise on me. "My car is parked in a lot behind the Ferris wheel. Come on with me, I have something for you. Stay here, Berta, I'll be right back."

I followed him to the car, a Ford Fairlane. He opened the trunk, removed a briefcase, and took his wallet from the briefcase. "At the beach I'm afraid of pickpockets." He handed over ten dollars.

"After Roldán left I started feeling guilty," he explained. "I don't know why. One morning I woke up asking myself, Whatever happened to that quiet gringo? I never went to your apartment, I didn't have an address or a phone number, and I don't even know your real name. But I said, Maybe one day I'll see him. So look—here we are. A miracle. At last my conscience can rest. Isn't this a wonderful conclusion to our friendship?"

"Yes," I said. Then we embraced warmly and disappeared forever from each other's lives.

Occasionally I spied Chuy on the Greenwich Village streets, but without a connection through the empanada stand we had little to say to each other. Once, when I asked him about Cathy Escudero, he replied, "Who?" So I explained. He said, "Oh, that cute girl went to Uruguay, but they never got married. He ditched her for an aristocrat. Who knows what happened next?"

I saw Carlos the Artist a final time, seated at an outdoor table in front of the Village Gate with his wife, sipping a planter's punch. Esther looked delicious in a low-cut peasant blouse and a tight skirt. Carlos had on a sport coat and tie, his hair was in a crew cut, and he'd shaved off the handlebar mustache. "I decided to look *really* weird, blondie." They were headed for Paris, then Bonn, Germany. In each city he would have a one-man show. I said congratulations, we embraced fondly, and he was gone with the rest.

For a while the old gang seemed out of my life forever. Yet on a busy late-summer afternoon I met Gino on Sullivan Street. He was impeccably attired as always and asked immediately, "Have you got a girlfriend?"

"No, not yet I'm afraid."

He laughed. "Jesus, I don't understand you, kid. This city is like a rain forest full of beautiful pibas out there for the choosing. There's quetzal birds and cockatoos, pericos and oropéndolas, and magnificent birds of paradise. All you have to do is whistle."

But he was in a hurry with many things to do and people to meet so we didn't chat for long. Gino tipped his Borsalino, we shook hands and embraced, and then off he went in an important slither of silk, bound for the money, I'm sure.

63. Memory Lane

I couldn't hang on in New York any longer. I was too broke and still unpublished after a year of trying. I was very discouraged. Time to find a real job in a smaller pond among friends and family members. Sayonara, Broadway. So long, Herald Square.

My last act before I quit the city was a trip up memory lane to Fourteenth Street and then west to Eighth Avenue. It was a sunny September afternoon when all the girls of Manhattan were still dressed in tight jerseys and short skirts and they looked like cotton candy. People were gathered around Sabrett hot-dog wagons buying wieners and soda pop. A few men in shirtsleeves listened to the Yankees on transistor radios.

First I stood on the sidewalk outside the old building staring up at the studio windows, all of which were open. Then I went in the foyer and climbed to the fourth floor instead of taking the elevator. I went down the corridor to the right door and tried the handle—it was unlocked. So I pushed it open, entering the empty studio. I shut the door behind me and remained still for a minute facing myself in a mirror. Then I sat down at my old spot far from where Jorge and Cathy Escudero used to practice and I waited for a while. Jorge's chair was gone. It was warm and cheerful street noises came through the open windows. I heard a faint tapping of Cathy's flamenco shoes in rhythm to whispery arpeggios from a guitar. Ghostly and beautiful, Cathy swished her skirt back and forth, frowning like a fierce little bird of prey with tragic joy and arrogance. Jorge remained an adolescent boy under the porkpie hat, but oh what a marvelous player he was. They had worked so hard to be wonderful.

Eventually I grew afraid that somebody would enter the room and be surprised by me, the unwanted intruder. So I got up and went away. When I stopped at the Downtown Café the friendly waitress with pretty green eyes came over. "Well, well," she said, "long time no see. What'll it be today—coffee?"

I ordered my java black and had a glazed doughnut, dabbing the pastry into my steaming cup before every bite. The restaurant was busy and the sidewalk was crowded also. On my napkin I wrote, Con alma ardiente, el cuerpo nunca se cansa. I wrote it three times in a row, then turned over the napkin and did the same thing again on the other side. If the soul is on fire, the body never gets tired.

When I raised my eyes the waitress was standing there with an inquisitive look on her face. "I don't mean to pry," she said, "but how did your story turn out?"

"They went away to be married," I said. "The dancer and Liberace. For me it's a sad story." I didn't want to tell her about Jorge, though, so I asked, "How's Bobby? Did you get him out of jail?"

Her eyes widened in delight and she gave me a big fat grin. "You remember Bobby? Oh my goodness. How did you remember him?"

"I'm a trained professional," I said.

She laughed, and I did too. Then she looked at her watch and said, "Hey, do you have plans, or would you like to go for a walk? My shift is over in fifteen minutes."

I almost declined her invitation, but said instead, "Okay, if you want."

She brought me a *Daily News* and a *Journal-American* that customers had discarded. I read them until she clocked out and figured her tips. Together we walked east on Fourteenth Street to Sixth Avenue, then down to Washington Square. She admitted that she'd never had a boyfriend named Bobby, and he hadn't been arrested for stealing tires, either. When she made up stories to share with customers the time passed more quickly.

The evening in Washington Square was serene. We sat on a bench and talked.

Her name was Irene Dupree, not her real name, she had invented it when she came to Manhattan from Cincinnati three years ago. She was twenty-eight. Her four-year-old son, John, lived in Ohio with his dad, whose name was Doug. She had a serious alcohol problem but was working on it. Aside from being a waitress, she also did occasional secretarial jobs for a temp service that provided businesses with girls like herself who could type and act intelligent. At night, twice a week, she attended an academy I had never heard of, studying to be a nurse.

"I like to help people when they're feeling down and out. I've been there myself."

Her outfit was nondescript. A green blouse, a modest skirt, and saddle shoes. She had been a high-school cheerleader and really loved to dance. She could do cha-cha and mambo and the Charleston; she could jitterbug and was learning tango. What did I think of Rudolph Valentino? She liked movies; her favorite actresses were Natalie Wood and Eva Marie Saint. Had I seen *Splendor in the Grass* or *On the Waterfront*?

Irene wanted to visit my apartment. I balked. "It's just a little pigpen," I said.

"I don't mind." She took my hand and pulled me up off the bench. "I'll only stay a minute. You don't have to walk me home."

We detoured off West Broadway so I could show her where the empanada stand had been. I told her about Roldán and my friend Alfonso, and Luigi with his burnt face. I wondered if Roldán was right now at the beach in San Sebastián drinking a rum and Coke.

She said her father worked as a ticket agent at the Cincinnati railroad station. Her mother taught people how to teach braille to the blind. She had two sisters, Kerry and Melissa, and a brother, Dave, who'd earned a football scholarship to Wayne State, in Indiana.

"I'm the black sheep of the family. I've even had an abortion."

At West Broadway and Prince Street I opened my mailbox. There was a sealed letter for me from the seventh publisher on my list, and another envelope from my draft board. However, I didn't want to open either of them in front of a stranger.

After we climbed up to my apartment I boiled some water and made two cups of instant coffee. We sat at my tin table painted to resemble wood. From her bitten-down fingernails the polish was flaking off. She had little pearls in her earlobes. One shoelace was untied. "I buy most of my clothes at the Salvation Army or Goodwill Industries or other secondhand places. If you're selective, cheap things can look real nice."

She lived in a building not far away, on Morton Street. Her apartment was about the size of mine, she told me, except the toilet was down a hallway beside the communal shower. She did sit-ups in her bedroom and walked all over New York unafraid of being mugged. In high school she had also played softball, a pitcher on the team.

My manuscripts littering the floor intrigued her. "How can you write a book? It seems like the most impossible thing to do." She used to read a lot but not anymore, except for the nursing texts. She didn't like the Bible. Norman Vincent Peale was okay. As a kid she read Nancy Drew. She remembered *Kiss Me Deadly*, by Mickey Spillane, because it had scared her half to death. A friend of hers at school, Dorothy, had an uncle who'd been murdered during the robbery of a toy store, shot with a .22.

Irene Dupree stood up and tiptoed through my manuscripts to check out my shelves of books. She read the titles aloud and asked me about the authors. Then she took off her shoes and invited me to lie down beside her on the bed. We held each other until gradually she quit talking. I hardly said a word, I was so surprised and afraid. After a while she kissed me and then we made love.

Of course I remember every detail of what transpired. I remember how her body was and the sensations I experienced and what we said to each other. But that seems private here. Somehow I had stumbled into the astonishing realm of sex when I least expected it.

And then my world changed in ways that I never could have imagined.

Epilogue: How to Eat an Empanada

Many years have passed, and I never again heard from any of those boys and girls at the empanada stand. Yet I still have a dream that one day Alfonso might track me down, showing up at my door as promised with the pragmatic Sofía on his arm and three handsome kids in tow, and the ratty purple scarf tossed loosely around his neck.

This is how I have always envisioned the moment:

"Hola, profe, qué hacés?" I say, and he throws his arms around me.

"Che, blondie—how the heck are you doing?"

They step inside and meet my first wife and pat the dog and shake hands with our two young children. After that, Alfonso produces a greasy paper bag and reaches inside, removing empanadas made of beef and quince and cheese and chicken and raisins. We turn on a burner under a pot of oil and drop them in. My wife runs off to buy wine, Tabasco sauce, and ice cream for dessert. While she is gone I open a trunk full of old manuscripts and locate a parcel containing the two pieces of Áureo Roldán's plaster of Paris cast with all the greetings and signatures on it. Carefully, I unwrap this artifact and put it in the center of our dining room table, replacing the bowl of fruit. Between both halves of the cast I arrange a tall candle and light it.

Then we sit down at the table and, with a baroque flourish, Alfonso distributes the steamy empanadas. My daughter and her brother frown suspiciously at the hot little pies on their plates.

"This is how to eat an empanada," Alfonso explains, picking one up and wrapping the bottom half with a paper napkin. He proceeds to nip off the top and splash on the Tabasco. After that he takes a good bite and chews for a while, savoring the delicious taste with his eyes closed, remembering how exquisite the empanadas tasted when we were desperately poor.

I pour the wine. A cheap bottle from Chile, so popular nowadays. And we lift our glasses, tapping them together as we proclaim in cheerful Spanish:

"Health, love, money . . . and all the time in the world to spend them!"